I0679147

Led by Her Heart

Katelyn Marie Peterson

2023, Amore Moon Publishing
TWB Press

Led by Her Heart
Book One - A Lynn Callahan Romantic Suspense

Copyright © 2023 by Katelyn Marie Peterson

All rights reserved. No part of this story may be reproduced or transmitted in any form or by any means, electronic or mechanical, including photocopying, recording, or by any information storage and retrieval system, without written permission of the author, except in the case of brief quotations embodied in critical articles or book reviews.

This is a work of fiction. Names, characters, places, and incidences are either a product of the author's imagination or are used fictitiously. Any resemblance to any actual person, living or dead, events, or locales is entirely coincidental.

Edited by Terry Wright

Cover Art by Terry Wright
Image from shutterstock.com

ISBN: 978-1-959768-30-2

Dedication:

For my beloved mother and biggest fan,
Patricia Peterson

Chapter 1

Lynn Callahan sat back in her desk chair and stared at her office wall clock. Her knee bounced rapidly, and her fingers tapped vigorously against her walnut desktop. She was supposed to meet with a prospective client at three, but the woman called to say she was running late.

"I ran into traffic on the way over," she had said. "I should be there in ten minutes." That was fifteen minutes ago.

Traffic Shmaffic. Mama needs to go home.

Ordinarily she was a patient person. Being a full-time working single parent to a rambunctious seven-year-old, patience was key. But tonight, she was a free agent. Her ex-husband, Drew, would have their son, Danny, for the weekend, and she had plans with her girlfriends. Dinner and drinks at eight, schmoozing, and late-night karaoke to follow. She needed time to go home and get ready: shower, change out of her pink silk blouse and grey trousers and into a loose-fitting V-neck and hip-huggers.

Staring at the clock was pointless. She pushed

herself up from her chair and walked to the window diagonal from her desk. The view from her Vermont office building was breathtaking. In the distance, scattered stands of pin cherry trees were set against a clear blue sky where a flock of birds soared by. She'd grown up in Vermont and lived in several of the state's cities, but Burlington was by far her favorite. Whether she was touring the Burlington Bike Path with her parents, exploring the shops at Church Street Marketplace with her friends, or simply gazing at Lake Champlain's beauty from Perkins Pier, there was always something for her to do.

Her musings were broken when her intercom chimed. "Your three o'clock is here." It was her assistant, Angela.

Finally.

"Send her in."

Violet Miller walked in. She was a little taller than Lynn, standing five-foot-five with short strawberry-blond hair and blue eyes. "I'm so sorry I'm late, Ms. Callahan."

"It's all right. Delays happen." She motioned to the armchair in front of her desk. "Have a seat."

Violet unzipped her brown leather jacket and draped it on the back of the chair.

Lynn sat behind her desk. "I'm curious. How did

you find out about Callahan's Party Planning?"

"My best friend, Cassie Ferguson. Your company planned her baby shower. She specifically dropped your name."

"Yes. I remember Cassie. I'm happy she was so pleased."

"And I was very impressed. I especially loved the centerpieces."

Lynn had made several contacts over the years, one of them being a wood carver. She'd asked him for baby-themed centerpieces and the result was a set of ducklings painted yellow and blue with the expected due date carved on the bottom.

"I understand you are looking to hire someone to plan a surprise party."

"For my mother, Lydia. She's turning sixty."

"I've planned a lot of birthday parties. My specialty." She opened her middle desk drawer and pulled out a big binder. "This is my portfolio."

As Violet was looking through the binder, Lynn's cell phone rang. She was prepared to ignore the call until she looked down and saw that it was from Danny's school. Her heart thumped with a jolt of concern. *They never call...*

She looked up at Violet. "I need to take this." She rushed out of her office then answered the call.

"Hello?"

"Ms. Callahan." It was the principal. "Danny is still here waiting to be picked up."

A shot of adrenaline lit fires in her bloodstream. "His dad was supposed to—"

"We've called Mr. Callahan but haven't been able to reach him."

That wasn't like Drew. He was always reliable, especially when it came to Danny.

"I'm on my way."

She rushed back into her office. "I'm so sorry, Violet. I need to cut our meeting short."

"Oh. How much for this special package?" She pointed to a page in the binder.

"Seven hundred fifty dollars."

"That's fine. I want to hire you."

"Wonderful. Have Angela set up another meeting for us to go over all the details." Lynn took her purse and white trench coat off the door hook and followed Violet out of the office. They'd made it to the middle of the lobby when she heard her name being called with urgency.

"Lynn. Lynn. Wait up."

She turned around to see Cassidy Kincaid, her young new hire, rushing down the hall, dodging other employees. Her bushy brown ponytail flailed from side to side.

When Cassidy reached Lynn, she was out of breath. "It's a disaster...a disaster...we have a crisis...a crisis on our hands."

"Cassidy, slow down. Tell me what happened."

"The band for the Powell party quit. It's next week, Lynn."

"I don't get it. They're our party staple. Why did they quit?"

"I don't know. I called all the local bands...on our backup list...all I could reach. No one...no one is available on short...short notice. It's a disaster." Her blue eyes were wide with panic.

"Cassidy, breathe. In..." Lynn demonstrated. "And out. It's not a disaster. These things happen. There are plenty of DJs in the area—"

"But Mrs. Powell wants a live band."

"At this point, a DJ is her only option. Call Mrs. Powell and explain the situation. Tell her you'll make sure the DJ knows what kind of music she wants."

"Okay. Yeah. I'll call her now."

"Before you do, take a minute to collect yourself. And remember, sound like you have confidence in yourself."

Cassidy swallowed hard. "Easy for you to say."

"Go."

She rushed off toward her cubicle.

Crisis averted.

When Lynn stepped out of the building, she was met with an April breeze that made her auburn curls dance. Drew had better have a damn good reason for not showing up at school. Lingering adrenaline caused her hand to shake as she tucked a few strands of hair behind one ear. She nearly dropped her key fob as she fumbled with the buttons to unlock the door of her Honda Pilot. Once she was in the car, she dialed Drew.

Pick up the phone. Pick up the phone. Pick up the phone.

The call went to voicemail. A chunk of granite formed in the pit of her stomach. "Drew, I'm on my way to pick up Danny. Call me."

As she careened the car into the flow of traffic on Prospect, she contemplated Drew's sudden absence. He was either in the hospital—on a ventilator, unable to call—or he was dead. There were no other acceptable excuses for failing to pick up his son.

She prayed it was neither.

Chapter 2

*T*raffic *Smaffic.* No wonder Violet was late. The route to Danny's school was stop-and-go-slow all the way down Main. When she finally arrived, parked the car, and rushed to the front entrance, she found Danny and the principal standing in the doorway. "I'm so sorry about this, sir."

"I hope Mr. Callahan is okay. It's not like him to be late." He looked down at Danny. "See you on Monday."

"Bye." As he followed his mom toward the car, he asked, "Is Daddy mad at me?"

Her heart broke a little at that question. "No, honey. Of course not." When they reached the car, she knelt and drew him into a hug then kissed the top of his head. "He loves you so much. We both do."

"I know." He pulled away from her, opened the car door, threw his backpack on the seat, and climbed inside. "But why isn't he here? Why isn't he answering his phone?" His eyebrows were pulled close together, and tears were beginning to well in his big brown eyes. "I got scared..." he sobbed, "waiting."

She stroked his wavy brown hair as she waited for him to get buckled in. "I wish I had an answer for you, bud. But I know this much. Daddy is not mad at you."

Danny crossed his arms and lowered his head. "I wanna go home."

There wasn't anything she could say to make him feel better, but she knew one thing for sure. *I have to find Drew.*

She got in the driver's seat, took her phone out, and sent a group message to the girls. *'Change of plans for tonight. I can't make it.'*

Lisa responded in rapid fashion: *'No way. What's going on?'*

Valerie was quick to follow with, *'It won't be the same without you, girlfriend.'*

No response from Melanie. Lynn knew to expect a call. *Five, four, three, two...*

The phone rang. *Yup. Melanie.* Lynn was in for an earful. She answered, mentally cursing Drew for screwing up her plans. "Melanie, I'm sorry."

"Lynn, what the hell? I've been looking forward to seeing you all week. I've got a new outfit to show you. We need our girl-time, girl."

Lynn felt terrible as she pictured Melanie's caramel eyes crinkling and her lower lip pouting out.

Led by Her Heart

"I wouldn't cancel if it weren't important. But I need your help...with Danny."

"Danny? What's wrong with him?"

"Can I bring him to your house right now?"

"Right now? I'm getting ready to go out."

"Forget about clubbing, drinking, cute guys, all of it. This is an emergency."

"Crap. Alright. I'll leave the door open."

"See you in ten."

Melanie was many things: funny, feisty, annoying at times, but she was also the best friend Lynn could ever ask for. They'd met when she was pregnant with Danny. Craving a chocolate chip cookie, she saw an ad for the Sweets All Around Café. She walked in for a simple cookie and came out with an irreplaceable friendship.

**

Lynn hadn't yet put her car in park when she heard Danny unlatch his seat belt. "Daniel Jeremiah Callahan. How many times have I told you to wait until the car is off before you unfasten your seat belt?"

Danny shrugged. "Can I get out now?"

She put the car in park, turned it off, and let out a frustrated sigh. "Go ahead."

Melanie stepped out of her vinyl-sided gray cape and walked down the steps of her front porch to greet

~9~

them. "Hey, kiddo." She scooped up Danny in her arms.

"Hi, Aunt Melanie," he said in a muffled tone then swiped a few strands of her long blond hair off his face.

She giggled and set him down. Once they were inside, Melanie knelt to Danny. "Do you feel like helping me bake some chocolate chip cookies?"

"Yay." He started jumping up and down. "To sell them in your bakery?"

"Maybe. Why don't you head in the kitchen and put on the apron I left for you on the chair."

Melanie waited until Danny was out of earshot, then she turned her attention to Lynn. "Okay, what the hell's going on?"

"I'm worried about Drew. He didn't show up to get Danny from school, and he hasn't been answering his phone."

"That doesn't sound like him."

"I'm going to drive to his apartment, see if he's home. If he's not, I'll have to check the hospitals and the police department."

"Do what you need to do. Danny and I will be fine."

"You're the best friend ever."

"Tell that to the hunk I could have met tonight."

Lynn waved her off, got in the car, closed her eyes, and took a deep breath. Her mind wandered to the worst-case scenario: Drew's lifeless body in the morgue, soon followed by an excruciating conversation with Danny about his dad never coming home. *No. He's fine. He's home, sleeping. His phone battery is dead. That's all it is.*

Chapter 3

Lynn fretted all the way to Drew's apartment. They may have been divorced, but he was Danny's father and someone she still cared about. They'd met fifteen years ago, during their sophomore year of college. She recognized right away that Drew was someone worth knowing. He was confident without being cocky, smart but not pretentious, and he was genuinely nice to everyone he met. When she found out about his drug addiction— after showing up at his dorm and catching him red-handed, snorting cocaine with his roommate, Dale Hogan—she was already too emotionally invested to simply walk away.

She'd stuck with him through it all: the withdrawals, the rehabs, the relapses, but when she found out she was pregnant with Danny, she'd given him an ultimatum. *Get clean or get out.*

Now, though the romance was gone, her friendship with Drew remained, and she would always care about him.

When she pulled into the parking lot of his

apartment building, she saw that his blue Subaru Outback wasn't in its parking spot. A lump formed in the back of her throat. *His car is gone. He's not answering his phone. Maybe he... No.* She pushed that wedge of doubt out of her mind. *He didn't relapse. Something else is going on.*

With nervous fingers, she struggled to unlatch her seatbelt, as her mind raced, plaguing her with unspeakable scenarios. *Is he lying unconscious on the bathroom floor? But why is his car gone? Was he the victim of a home invasion, shot dead for his TV, X-Box, and his car? I need to get into that apartment.* Finally free from her seatbelt, she piled out, slammed her car door shut, and rushed into Drew's apartment building. The elevator took forever to get up to the third floor.

Finally at his door, she knocked a couple of times before she reached into her purse and pulled out the spare key he had given to her for emergencies. When she walked in, the apartment was quiet: no music, no television, no shower running.

"Drew?" She gripped the leather strap of her purse.

In the living room, at first glance, nothing seemed out of place. Two blankets were neatly draped over the back of the sofa. Family photos were undisturbed on each end-table, and the fifty-five-inch flat-screen was still mounted to the wall. Beneath it was a small entertainment unit that housed the X-Box and a glass-encased, signed Steelers football helmet.

She was making her way to Drew's bedroom when her foot nudged something on the floor, his cell phone. The discovery robbed her of her next breath. He'd never willingly go anywhere without his phone. *Why is it on the floor? He has to be here somewhere.* As she had watched enough cop shows to know potential evidence when she saw it, she stepped around the phone and headed down the hallway.

When she entered his bedroom, her disbelieving eyes landed on two empty prescription pill bottles on his nightstand next to a framed picture of him and Danny. Her legs became rubber, and the room started to spin.

No. This can't be. They're not his.

She'd lived with Drew's addiction for years and learned to recognize the signs of a relapse. He was in a good place. He wasn't acting irritable or stressed out; he wasn't acting irresponsibly; his behavior was the same as it had been since he'd gotten clean. The pill bottles told a story, but not Drew's.

She scanned his bedroom. The bed was made, all his dresser drawers were shut, and the laptop on a small desk in the corner was untouched.

On the nightstand on the other side of the bed, stood a framed picture of Drew and a woman, probably the new girlfriend he'd recently mentioned, standing on a dock at Lake Champlain. The sky was clear blue, the sun shining down on scattered sailboats cutting wakes beyond the couple. Drew had his arm around the woman. His warm brown eyes were focused on the camera while he tilted his head toward the woman. His shaggy brown hair touched her shoulder-length honey-blond locks. She was hugging his waist. Her wide smile reached her hazel eyes, which seemed to be saying, "He's mine now, ladies."

He looks so happy...like he'd been with his ex-girlfriend, Theresa.

The picture confirmed what she knew in her heart. Drew was happy. He was clean. He had to be in some kind of trouble, by someone else's actions.

She left the bedroom to check the bathroom and then the kitchen. Danny's bedroom looked like a bomb had gone off in there. Nothing was taken, everything was in its place, aside from the pill bottles.

Stay calm.

She took her phone out of her purse, then walked back into the living room and sat on the couch. Aside from herself, there were two people who knew Drew just as well as she did, starting with his mother, Andrea. That would be a fun call to make. *Not!*

Since the divorce, Andrea hated Lynn, despite it being a mutual decision between her and Drew. "How can you be so selfish?" she had said. "In sickness and in health, or does my son mean that little to you? And what about *your* son? Clearly you haven't thought of Danny at all."

The phone rang a few times before Andrea answered. "What do you want, Lynn?"

Just the greeting she'd expected. Two years after the divorce, Andrea was still nursing the same bitter grudge.

"Andrea, please listen. It's about—"

"I can't believe you would ever call me about anything. Clearly you didn't get the message when I said—"

"It's Drew."

"Wh-what? Is he okay?"

"He's missing."

"Missing? How?"

"That's what I'm trying to find out. When was the last time you spoke to him?"

"A couple days ago. He and Danny are coming over for lunch tomorrow. Maybe he's at the movies." Her voice cracked.

"Drew didn't show to pick Danny up from school, and he hasn't been answering his phone. I found it on the floor in his living room."

"Oh, God. He never goes anywhere without his phone." Her breathing became rapid and shallow. "Could he have relapsed again?"

Don't tell her about the pill bottles.

"Andrea, listen to me. He's been clean for eight years."

"You're...you're right." Her breathing slowed down. "Have you called the cops?"

"Not yet. I'm going to call Charlie first."

"Good. Good. But what if he hasn't heard from him either?"

"I'll keep you updated."

"Wait, Lynn...you have Danny, right?"

"He's with Melanie."

Andrea inhaled deeply. "I still want him to come for lunch tomorrow."

"Of course. I'll drop him off."

Lynn ended the call and immediately pulled up Charlie Benson in her contacts. He was Drew's best friend and colleague at the University of Vermont. He answered on the second ring. "Charlie, it's Lynn Callahan."

"Lynn," he said guardedly. "To what do I owe

the pleasure?"

"Have you heard from Drew?

"Ah...yesterday, after work. We were supposed to grab dinner, but he canceled, said he'd be up late grading papers."

"So...did he come into work this morning?"

"As a matter of fact, he called in sick. What's going on?"

Her heart began to pound, and she started to feel dizzy with dread. She placed Charlie on speaker then put the phone down next to her, leaned her head back against the couch, and closed her eyes. "Drew was supposed to pick up Danny from school, but he didn't show up, and he's not answering his calls."

"Maybe he lost his phone."

"I'm at his apartment now. His car is gone, and his phone is here."

"Maybe his mom has heard from him."

"She's worried that he may have started using again."

"No way. He just showed me his eight-year chip last week. He's dedicated to his sobriety. You should call the police."

"After I call the hospital."

Charlie exhaled sharply. "I hope he's alright."

"If you hear from him, call me."

"I will." He hung up.

She picked up her phone and stared at the screen, preparing for what she might hear during her next call.

"UVM Medical Center."

"Has Drew Callahan been admitted to your hospital?"

"Are you family?"

"He's my ex-husband, and he's missing. Our son is sick with worry. Please..."

"Let me check." Fingers clicked on a keyboard, then, "No one by that name is here."

"Thank goodness."

"I hope you find him alright."

"Thank you." She hung up and clutched the phone to her heart. Relief and angst battled in her chest.

She sighed. *On to the next dreaded call. I'm ready to wake up from this nightmare. Anytime now, Lord.*

***

Lynn was nervous enough before she called the cops, but when she looked out of Drew's window and saw a squad car pull up in front, her nerves kicked into high gear. Her heart started to pound, and a heaviness formed in her chest, as if it were the stomping ground for an elephant herd.

Great. Drew's MIA, and I'm about to have a heart attack.

She held the door open as two uniformed officers stepped off the elevator. One was tall with broad shoulders and had dark brown hair and brown eyes. The other one was older, on the shorter side and was going bald.

"Ms. Callahan?" the taller officer asked.

"Please, come in." She closed the door behind them and led them into the living room.

The tall one started off. "My name is Officer Diaz, and this is my partner, Officer Grayson." He motioned to the balding man. "It's not often we get a call about a missing University Professor. Sarge sent us right away."

"I'm worried sick."

"Grayson's going to look around while I get some information from you." He took a notepad and pen from his shirt pocket.

Officer Grayson began his search while Lynn and Officer Diaz sat on the living room couch. Hoping she had helpful information, she watched as he flipped his notepad open and readied his pen. "How long has your ex-husband been missing?"

"He was supposed to pick up our son from school this afternoon, but he didn't show."

Diaz jotted that down. "And no word from him?"

"His colleague, Charlie Benson, told me he called in sick, but as you can see, he's not here."

"Charlie Benson..." He wrote on his pad. "And that's out of character for him?"

"Absolutely. Drew's never late for anything."

"How about a girlfriend? Maybe he ran off to Vegas for the weekend. Wouldn't be the first time we'd seen it. Might very well show up on Monday morning, heavily tanned and hung over."

She didn't want to believe that could happen in a million years, but... "He has a girlfriend, but I doubt he'd take off like that...abandon his son at school...not Drew. They had plans for the weekend."

"What's the girlfriend's name?"

"I don't know her. There's a picture of him and her in the bedroom."

"Can I borrow it?"

"Maybe this one would be better." She turned to the end-table and lifted a framed photo of Drew and Danny at Disney World. They were standing in front of the castle, wearing matching Disney shirts. At 6-foot-4-inches, Drew looked like a giant compared to Danny. His sunglasses were pushed back over his hair, and his wide smile created lines beneath his eyes.

Lynn did her best to hold back tears, but one

resisted her every effort. She turned the frame over and took the photo out then handed it to him. "Be careful with it."

"I'll make a copy and get it back to you." He took the picture then nodded to the floor. "Is that his cell phone?"

"It was lying there when I came in. I didn't touch it."

Officer Diaz stood, pulled a white cloth from his cargo pants pocket, bent down, and used it to pick up the phone. "I'll have to get a search warrant to go through this."

"How long will that take?"

"Tomorrow, probably." He put the phone in an evidence bag, also from his pants pocket. "Detectives will want to look through it." He returned to the couch. "Is there anyone in Drew's life that may want to hurt him?"

"Drew's a very friendly guy. As far as I know, he's gets along well with everyone at work...the University of Vermont."

"Any vices we should be aware of, gambling, drinking?"

"He's a recovering addict, been clean for eight years."

"Are you sure?"

She recalled the empty prescription bottles. "Yes. I'm sure."

Officer Grayson walked out of Drew's bedroom. He motioned for Diaz to join him in the hall. There was indistinct chatter before both officers came back to the living room.

Grayson looked at Lynn. "Ma'am, did you see these in the bedroom?" He held up the empty pill bottles.

She swallowed hard. "I did."

Diaz frowned. "You said you were sure he was clean. The pill bottles seem to say otherwise."

Lynn shook her head adamantly. "I know how this looks, but I'm telling you Drew is clean. He just got his eight-year chip last week."

Officer Grayson placed the pill bottles on the kitchen counter. "Has he relapsed before?"

"Yes. But like I said, he's been clean for eight years."

"Addiction is a powerful disease. Anything could trigger a setback."

"I know how addiction works, Officer. I watched Drew struggle with it for years. If he was having problems, he would have told me."

Officer Diaz came back to the couch. "Ma'am, we're not discounting Drew's efforts to stay clean, but you're the last person he would tell."

Grayson said, "It's very likely his addiction got the better of him, and he doesn't want to be found. It would explain why his car is missing and his phone is here."

"Or he got himself involved in a drug deal gone bad," Diaz added.

Lynn tried to remain calm, but their words angered her. She could feel her face getting hot. "Are you saying you're not going to look for Drew?"

Officer Grayson groaned. "Ms. Callahan, I promise this will be treated like any other case. We'll write up a missing persons report, get it out to the media along with a full description of Drew's car. You just need to prepare yourself for all possible outcomes."

"He hasn't relapsed. I know Drew. He wouldn't do that."

Diaz returned Drew's phone to Lynn.

She scrunched her eyebrows together. "I-I thought you needed his phone. You said the detectives would want to go through it."

"Given this new information, I don't think that will be necessary." He flipped out a business card. "When he shows up, call me. I'd like to have a word with him."

"We'll let you know if we hear anything," Grayson said.

The officers walked out and closed the door with a thud.

Lynn collapsed to the floor, cross-legged, and buried her head in her hands, tears now streaming down her face. They said they'd look for him, but how hard would they try? To them, Drew was just a wayward drug addict on a bender somewhere, maybe in Las Vegas. They'd already made up their minds, but she knew better.

She reached for her purse and took out a tissue to wipe her face. She imagined she looked like a hot mess: tear-stained cheeks, puffy green eyes, red nose.

After cleaning herself up, she placed her phone, and Drew's, in her purse, and stood up from the floor. She headed into the kitchen to throw the tissue away then walked to the counter where Officer Grayson had placed the pill bottles. She picked them up and examined them closely. The medication on the prescription label read, Oxycodone, but the patient's name had been scraped off. *'No Refills.'*

No way they could be Drew's.

She walked to the bedroom where she took Drew's laptop off his desk. There had to be something in here or on his phone that would prove her instincts were right.

Drew was in trouble. Those pill bottles had something to do with his disappearance, alright, a red herring to throw off any missing person investigation. He didn't relapse. So, who put them there, and more importantly, where was Drew now?

Chapter 4

On the drive back to Melanie's house, Lynn's stomach rumbled with a forceful consistency. She hadn't eaten anything since lunch. The sound of her hungry stomach distracted her from the worry she'd been feeling for Drew.

When she pulled into Melanie's driveway, Lynn wondered what she would tell Danny if he asked about his dad. She had no updates, minus his missing car and the cops' relapse theory.

She'd stick with the half-truth: 'Daddy wasn't home, but his phone was. He probably left in a hurry and forgot to take it with him.'

That'll do.

As she walked to Melanie's open front door, Lynn sniffed the air. Something smelled delicious, a combination of pasta and garlic. When she walked into the house, Danny rushed to her.

"Mommy." He wrapped his skinny arms around her waist.

"Hey, bud." She gave him a squeeze and kissed the top of his head.

Melanie sauntered out of the kitchen. "So, how'd it go?"

Danny let go of her waist. "Did you see Daddy? Is he mad at me?" His eyes were wide with worry.

Half-truth time.

"No. His phone was at the apartment though. He must have gone out and forgotten it."

Good job.

"Oh." He had little-boy curiosity on his face. "Where did he go?"

Melanie interjected, "Hey, Danny. Feel like drawing us a cool picture?"

"Yeah."

She led him to her desk in the corner of the living room. "There's paper in the top drawer. Have fun, kiddo."

Once Danny was settled, Melanie and Lynn walked into the kitchen.

"You hungry?" Melanie asked.

Lynn pointed to her grumbling stomach. "Can't you hear it?"

Melanie giggled. "I'll take that as a yes." She opened the fridge and pulled out a foil wrapped baking dish. Then she placed it on the counter and opened the cabinet door directly above her and reached for a dinner plate.

Lynn smiled when Melanie took the foil off. Her nose was right: broccoli cavatelli with a side of garlic bread.

"Help yourself to a drink." Melanie dished the bounty onto the plate. "So, what really happened at Drew's apartment?" she asked over the whir of the microwave.

Lynn sat at the kitchen table and opened the cap to the bottled water she'd taken from the fridge. "Nothing good." She swallowed a sip.

"Have you talked to your mom? She's usually your go-to person, aside from me, of course." She smiled slyly, as if she had one up on Lynn's mother.

"She and my dad are in Florida right now."

"That's right. I forgot about their cross-country road trip."

Lynn's dad had surprised her mom with a rented RV last week, a retirement gift. They were to travel around the country for three months. She couldn't remember the last time her parents took a vacation together, just the two of them. It was well deserved. "I want them to enjoy their vacation, not spend it worrying about us."

"Understandable. Now back to Drew. Lay it all on me."

"His car wasn't in the lot and his phone was on

the floor in his apartment."

"That doesn't sound good."

"It gets worse. There were two empty pill bottles on his nightstand."

"Oh, jeez." Melanie opened the microwave door and walked the plate to the table and set it in front of Lynn. "What kind of pills?"

"Oxy."

"No way. Did you report him as a missing person?"

"The cops think Drew relapsed, but I know he didn't." She chewed a piece of cavatelli, then took another sip of water. "Something else is going on."

"So, what are you going to do?"

Lynn sighed. "If the police won't look for Drew, I need someone who will...a private eye, maybe."

"Can you afford it? The cost can range anywhere from ninety-nine to one hundred fifty bucks an hour."

Lynn arched an eyebrow. "How do you know that?"

Melanie shrugged. "My parents have a very distrusting marriage, and yet, they're still married. Go figure."

Lynn laughed. "I have a rainy-day fund. That might cover the price." She finished off her cavatelli then carried her empty plate to the sink.

If dipping into her rainy-day fund meant finding Drew, she was all for it. Her one hope was that he'd be found. Alive.

Please be alive, Drew.

***

As she was driving home from Melanie's house, she listened to the soft sound of Danny snoring. In the rear-view mirror, she could see his head hung low and his mouth agape. She chuckled.

He always picks the worst time to fall asleep.

"Danny, honey. Wake up. We're home."

He moved his head up slowly and opened his eyes. "I wasn't sleeping," he said through a yawn.

"Oh, no? Just resting your eyes?"

"Uh huh."

Their puppy, Snowball, was watching them through the front window. He was perched on top of the living room couch. His front paws were on the windowsill, and he was barking louder than his size. He watched as she and Danny walked up the steps. When they entered through the front door of their blue raised ranch, Snowball leaped off the couch and ran straight to Danny, his tail wagging rapidly.

"Hi, Snowball." Danny took his jacket off and handed it to Lynn, then bent down and gently petted the top of the Bichon pup's head. "How you doing,

Snowball responded with several licks to Danny's right cheek.

Lynn smiled as she watched the two of them. They'd been thick as thieves since the day Snowball joined the family a year ago.

She walked into the kitchen and placed her purse and Drew's laptop on the table, hung Danny's coat on a chair, then walked back to Danny and Snowball. "Okay, bud, time for bed."

"Aw, can I stay up a little longer?"

She pointed to the living room wall clock. "It's almost nine. Sorry, kiddo. Past your bedtime."

"Okay. Can Snowball sleep in my room tonight?"

"Sure."

Once Danny was dressed and in bed, she grabbed a book from his bookshelf. With Snowball on the floor next to her feet, she began reading, *My Superhero Dad*.

By the last page, Danny was fast asleep. She got off his bed slowly then bent over to kiss his forehead and whisper, "Good night, sweetheart."

She picked up Snowball and placed him at the foot of Danny's bed. Then she closed the door and walked down the stairs and into the kitchen. She took Drew's phone out of her purse and placed it on his

~32~

laptop, then carried both into the living room where she curled up on the couch and set Drew's laptop next to her. His phone was PIN protected with Danny's birthday.

She searched through Drew's call history: Mom, Charlie, Lynn, Work, and several calls to and from a woman named Beth Meyers. She must have been the blonde in the photo on Drew's nightstand. There were no unknown numbers in the call history.

She inspected the laptop next. No alarming e-mails. No peculiar posts on his social media accounts. She clicked the message icon. Her eyes widened with alarm when she saw a conversation, five months back, between him and Dale Hogan, his college roommate and drug buddy.

Oh no. Not him.

She was nervous to read through the messages, but she needed all the insight she could get. Dale had reached out to Drew, saying how long it'd been since they'd hung out. *'We need to catch up. When are you free?'* But Drew rejected the invite, saying they weren't good for each other.

Good job.

Dale pushed, insisting that he was clean and that all he wanted to do was have dinner and talk, say his apologies, make amends, but Drew stayed firm. The conversation ended with, *'Fuck you, Callahan.'* She made a mental note of Dale's hostility. Anger was a powerful motivator to do harm to someone. It would definitely take a professional investigator to sort out that possibility.

Finished with the phone and laptop, she placed them on the coffee table and headed down the hall to her office. She took a seat at her desk, turned on her computer, and typed *private investigators near me* in the search engine.

Several names popped up, but if she wanted to find Drew, she needed the best of the best. Online reviews came in handy for that.

The first review was for L.P. Investigative Services. Three stars. "He was nice enough, but the cost was large and the outcome unreliable." His other reviews weren't as nice.

Not a chance.

Next, Moore P.I. Solutions. There were six reviews, all of them bad. "His attitude was gruff. His efforts lackluster," one review stated. Another one said, "He took my money, did not keep me updated. Results were inconclusive."

Lynn was losing hope until she scrolled upon Connolly Investigations. All rave reviews. "The cost was fair. Successful results," one said. Another, "He gave consistent updates and completed in less than a week." The rest of the reviews were just as flattering.

She clicked the link for the company's website. P.I. Jake Connolly graduated from the police academy fifteen years ago. He was a cop for eight years and a homicide detective for three years, until he was shot while in pursuit of a suspect. He'd opened Connolly Investigations two years ago.

Jake Connolly, he was the one. She added his phone number to her contact list and decided to call in the morning.

Hang in there, Drew. Wherever you are. Help is on the way.

Chapter 5

L ynn paced across her bedroom floor, her cell phone gripped in the palm of her hand. Danny was in the living room, watching cartoons, so now was the perfect time to call the P.I.

She took a seat at the foot of her bed and scrolled through her contact list until she reached *Connolly Investigations*. Her thumb hovered over the name, but the *what ifs* stalled her from initiating the call. What if she hired Connolly and still got nothing? Or worse yet, what if his investigation concluded with, "I'm so sorry for your loss."

I'll never know unless I try.

She took a deep breath then pressed the call button. The knots in her stomach tightened. The force traveled to her throat like strong hands wrapping around her neck.

"Connolly Investigations," a friendly woman's voice said. "How can I help you?"

The hold on Lynn's vocal cords loosened enough for her to speak. "My name is Lynn Callahan. Does Mr. Connolly have an opening? It's crucial that I meet with him as soon as possible."

"He can see you at three. Will that work for you?"

"That's perfect."

"You can save some time by filling out our client information form at connollyinvestigations.com."

"Yes. I've been there."

"We'll see you at three."

Lynn turned her gaze to the alarm clock on her nightstand: *10:30*. She had less than an hour and a half before she had to leave for Andrea's house to drop off Danny for lunch.

After completing the client form online, she walked to her bedroom door and opened it slightly. "Danny, honey, you need to get dressed," she called into the living room.

"Okay."

She closed the door again and got herself ready in a loose-fitting white t-shirt and pale blue jeans. Then she walked to her closet and took out a tote bag for Drew's laptop and phone just in case Connolly needed it.

She had her hand on her bedroom doorknob when Drew's phone in the tote bag started to ring. She fished it out and read the screen. *Beth Meyers*.

She contemplated whether to answer the call or

not, then: *Damn*. She answered but remained quiet.

"Drew? Drew, please say something." There was desperation in her voice.

Lynn felt a bit guilty for not being upfront.

"Drew. What's going on?"

"This is Lynn Callahan. I'm sorry he's not here."

"Drew's ex-wife? Why are you answering his phone?"

"Why are you calling him?"

"I'm his girlfriend. I've been trying to reach him since yesterday morning. Is he there with you?"

"No. He's—"

"Do you know where he is? I'm worried about him."

"He's, um...missing."

"Missing? No. No. What do you mean missing?"

"I don't know where he is. I filed a missing persons report yesterday."

She gasped. "The police? Okay. They'll find him. I'm sure."

Lynn exhaled deeply. "I wouldn't count on it."

"What are you talking about?"

"The cops think he relapsed, probably off somewhere doing drugs...maybe Las Vegas."

"What? No. That's crazy. Drugs? Why would they think that?"

Tread lightly.

"They know his history. He's relapsed before. In their mind, that's what this is."

She scoffed. "Certainly they're wrong."

"Beth, I think you're right, but have you noticed anything unusual about him lately?"

"Like what?"

"Has he seemed nervous? Moody? Maybe scared of someone?"

"What? No. Of course not. Wait. Don't tell me *you* believe Drew relapsed?"

She groaned, her patience wearing thin. "I didn't say that. I'm just trying to get all the facts together."

"Yeah, okay. Seriously. Am I the only one who believes in Drew?" She raised her voice. "You're his ex-wife, the mother of his child. You should know him better than anyone."

"Beth, I'm not the enemy here."

"Oh, no? Because it sure seems like—"

"Would you listen to me?" Lynn struggled to keep her voice steady. "I believe in Drew just as much as you do."

Beth scoffed.

"Look. Drew is in trouble, and he needs my help. The cops are useless so I'm hiring a private investigator."

Katelyn Marie Peterson

Silence on the line.

"Beth, are you still there?"

"Yeah. Yeah, okay." Her voice cracked. "Thanks. I um," she sniffled, "I need to go."

"It's going to be okay, Beth."

"You don't know that. How could you—?"

The line clicked dead. Lynn exhaled a long, shaky breath. That was the most awkward phone call she'd ever had. Now to follow that with a trip to see Drew's mother, the woman who hated her more than the devil himself.

**

Andrea was outside when Lynn and Danny arrived at her house. Her back was turned to them, her head down, as she tended to her garden, something she often did when she was stressed.

Lynn trailed behind Danny as he ran to Andrea.

"Grandma, Grandma," he yelled with excitement.

She turned as Danny leapt and threw his arms around her.

"Hi, sweetheart." She smiled and returned his monster-sized hug, then raised her head and gave Lynn a simple nod, her smile fading.

Danny spoke before Lynn had the chance to say anything. "What are we having for lunch, Grandma?"

Andrea chuckled as she removed her gardening

gloves. "I see how it is, young man. You come for the food. Grandma is just a bonus." She pushed her hands on the grass and levered herself up off the ground. "I'm going to make us BLTs with extra B for you."

Danny smiled wide. "And French Fries?"

"Of course."

Lynn gave Danny a kiss on the cheek. "Bye now. Have fun with Grandma, bud." She headed back to the car.

Andrea called out, "Lynn, wait."

She stopped, turned to look back, fully expecting another lecture. "What is it?"

Andrea removed her floppy hat, flicked a strand of blond hair away from her face, then looked down at Danny and back to Lynn. "Do you..?" She cleared her throat. "Would you like to stay for lunch with us?"

"Why? So you can badger me over a BLT?"

"Look. I'm doing my best here. It's awkward, but I need to talk to you."

"Just talk?"

"I promise."

"In that case, sure. Lunch would be nice."

Danny took the lead, running into the house. He tore off his orange and blue jacket and hung it in the hall closet, then he headed straight into the kitchen. "I'll get everything ready." He opened the fridge and grabbed the lettuce, tomato, and bacon. As he juggled the items to the counter, he gasped. "Oh, I almost forgot the mayo." He ran back to the fridge. "Silly me."

"Can't forget the mayo." Andrea pulled a loaf from the breadbox and set the oven to 'preheat' for the fries, and then she bent to open a low drawer to retrieve a baking pan and skillet. The burner came on and the bacon went in, then she loaded the pan with fries and popped them into the oven.

Lynn sat at the kitchen table as the aroma of frying bacon ballooned in the air. She wasn't sure what to say or do. The last time she was in Andrea's house was a few years ago, before the divorce.

"So, Lynn." Andrea kept her attention on the now sizzling bacon. "About that conversation we had yesterday. Any updates?"

She opened her mouth to respond but Danny beat her to it. "Are you talking about Daddy?"

Andrea laughed. "Sometimes I forget just how clever you are. Why don't you go watch TV while I get lunch ready."

Lynn waited until she heard the TV go on, then, "I talked to the cops. They're going to write up a missing persons report but..." She wondered if she should tell Andrea about the pill bottles. "I don't know how hard they're going to look for him."

"What? Why?" She turned the burner off and placed the bacon on a paper-towel-covered plate.

Lynn struggled for her next breath. "Truth be told, they, umm, found two empty pill bottles of Oxy on Drew's nightstand."

"Oh, God." Andrea turned around to face her. The color had drained from her cheeks. "Not again."

Lynn rushed to her. "Hey, listen to me." She placed both hands on Andrea's shoulders and looked straight into her eyes. "It doesn't matter what they found. Drew did not take those pills."

Andrea's whole body was shaking, and tears were streaming down her porcelain cheeks. "How do you know for sure? Let's not kid ourselves. No one is immune to a relapse on Oxy. He's had them before." Andrea pulled away to take the fries out of the oven.

"I just know. I can feel it in my heart."

"So, what now? We're just supposed to wait?"

"I'm meeting with a private investigator today at three."

Andrea shook her head and started putting the sandwiches together: sliced tomato, lettuce, and bacon, nice and crisp, all tucked between slices of lightly toasted bread. It was understandable that she had doubts. If the police didn't believe Drew was worth the effort, why would a P.I.?

"Jake Connolly has a promising success rate. I think he's our best shot at finding Drew."

Andrea cut the sandwiches in half and stacked them on a plate. "I hope you're right."

Lynn helped her carry the plates of sandwiches and fries to the table. "Danny, honey, lunch is ready."

"Yay." He ran into the kitchen, started to sit, then jumped back up. "Wait, we need ketchup."

Lynn snapped her fingers. "Can you get it for us, bud?"

"Mm-hmm. I'm on it." He dashed to the fridge.

Lynn swallowed a bite of her sandwich then whispered to Andrea. "Will you watch Danny while I meet with the P.I.?"

"Of course."

He rushed back to the table with the ketchup. "Alright, enough talking. Let's eat."

Lynn savored the taste of fresh tomatoes grown from Andrea's garden, which paired well with the crisp bacon. She always made the best BLT sandwiches. It was nice to be back in Andrea's kitchen, enjoying a nice meal and talking at normal volumes. However, lunch was bittersweet. The only reason

Andrea had invited her was because Drew was missing.

Her mind drifted to a dark place. Was Drew cold? Hungry? Struggling to stay alive? It took all her strength to not break down in front of Danny. She wanted to stay positive, but without knowing Drew's whereabouts, how could she?

Okay, P.I. Connolly. You're up.

Chapter 6

When Lynn arrived for her meeting with Jake Connolly, her stomach churned with nervous anticipation. She felt like she was about to throw up her lunch. She grabbed the tote bag, locked the car, and strode down a tree-lined sidewalk toward the impressive Courthouse Plaza building.

I need to get it together. He won't take the case if I vomit on him.

Her legs felt like Jell-O as she entered through the front glass doors. She scrolled through the directory in the center of the main lobby.

Connolly Investigations, third floor.

In the office atrium, a scent of lavender sweetened the air, and the faint sound of classical music played in the background.

"May I help you?" the receptionist asked.

"I'm Lynn Callahan. I have an appointment with Mr. Connolly at three."

The woman checked her computer screen. "I see your contact information is all here."

"I filled out your form online."

"Have a seat. He'll be right with you."

While she was waiting, she scrolled through photos in her phone. She had at least two hundred stored. Most of them were of her and Danny. It wasn't until she came across a photo of him and Drew that her eyes teared up. He was holding Danny as a newborn, their tiny bundle of joy. Drew hadn't seen Lynn take the picture. He was too focused on Danny: his perfect nose, velvety skin, and tiny toes. A reflection of beauty and innocence.

Oh, Drew. Where are you?

"Ms. Callahan."

She jumped a little when she heard a man's smooth voice call her name. "Here. I'm right here." She put her phone away and stood to face him.

"I'm sorry, Ms. Callahan. I didn't mean to startle you. I'm Jake Connolly."

He was slightly shorter than Drew, with brown hair combed up off his forehead, brown eyes, and a neatly trimmed beard.

She blinked away a tear. "I've been a little emotional lately."

"Perhaps I can help you with that." He topped the remark with a charming smile, one that nudged his cheekbones and revealed a cute set of dimples.

His demeanor gave her comfort. It was a nice

escape from her current distresses.

"Come on back."

She followed Jake into his spacious office. Immediately her attention was drawn to a gold frame that hung on the wall behind his desk, his P.I. certificate. More impressive were the awards honoring his law enforcement career. Investigative Excellence Award, Investigative Achievement Award, Outstanding Collaborative Investigation Award. There were also framed newspaper articles that acknowledged a few of his notable arrests.

"So, what brings you in today?" He pulled a plush armchair to his desk and offered it to her.

She sat, crossed one knee over the other, and set the tote bag next to the chair. "My ex-husband, Drew Callahan. He's been missing since yesterday morning. When I got to his apartment, his car was gone, and I found his phone on the floor in his living room. No one has seen or heard from him since Thursday."

"Did you call the police?"

"They said they would write up a report, but I'm afraid they're not going to look for him."

Jake frowned. "What makes you say that?"

She exhaled a shaky breath. "Drew is a recovering addict, eight years now. When I searched his apartment, I found two empty pill bottles. The cops think he relapsed and just took off."

Jake sighed. "That is a possibility, but you must have reason to believe that something else is going on."

"Drew loves his son more than anything. That's why he got clean in the first place."

"You might be right. Even if he did relapse, the father in him would eventually want to contact his son. Apologize, maybe."

"So, you believe there's another reason for him to be missing?"

"I can't say one way or the other. What do you want me to do for you?"

"I want you to find Drew, isn't it obvious?"

"I need you to be precise so we're both on the same page. No misunderstandings."

"So, you'll take the case then?"

"I'll look into it."

She felt like a weight had been lifted off her shoulders. "Thank you so much."

"Don't thank me yet. If I decide to take the case, I'll draw up a contract, set the scope of my investigation, and detail the charges."

"I understand. Anything you need. I'll pay anything."

"That's what they all say. First, I'd like to look

into his immediate circle. Is there anyone with a grudge? An angry co-worker? Bitter ex-girlfriend?"

"Dale Hogan," she said quickly. "He was Drew's college roommate. They partied together a lot."

"What makes you think Dale is involved in Drew's disappearance?"

"I looked through Drew's laptop. There were messages between him and Dale on one of his social media accounts. They didn't end well."

"How long ago was this?"

"Five months."

"What was the conversation about?"

"Dale wanted to see Drew, catch up, but Drew didn't want anything to do with him. He said Dale wasn't good for his sobriety."

"I take it that rejection made Dale angry."

"That would be an understatement."

"Dale Hogan." He wrote the name down on his notepad, then put the pen down. "It's a good starting place. Is there anyone else that I should know about?"

"There's an ex-girlfriend, Theresa Lambert. They broke up eight months ago, but I don't think she's bitter."

"Breakups can be very messy. Tell me what happened."

"Drew found out she had relapsed. He tried to

convince her to get help again, but she refused, so he ended things."

Jake put pen to notepad again. "Theresa Lambert, huh?"

"She has her issues, but I don't see her being involved in Drew's disappearance."

"You'd be surprised at what people do when exes are involved. Is he dating anyone new?"

"Beth Meyers. She called his phone earlier today, frantic about not hearing from him."

"That must have been awkward."

"She sounded worried. We didn't stay on the phone long. Drew's best friend, Charlie Benson would know about their relationship."

He added Beth and Charlie's names to his list, then put his pen back down. "Anything else?"

She took Drew's phone and laptop out of her tote bag and placed them on Jake's desk. "You can look through these, see if anything stands out."

"Great. They'll come in handy if I decide to take the case."

"Please, Mr. Connolly. I'm desperate."

"They all are. If you think of anyone else who might have motivated your ex to go missing, give me a call." He took a business card from a silver holder on the desk and handed it to her. "I'll be in touch."

Back in her car, she let out a deep breath. Jake Connolly. He was something else, the way he exuded confidence and professionalism, but his effect on her went beyond his skills as a P.I. Her mind drifted to a place of sensuality and seduction.

If she'd met him under different circumstances, she may well have fallen into his arms and explored the strength of his embrace and the softness of his lips. However, as fate would have it, he was all business and showed no particular interest in her. Only a moment's glance at her crossed knees showed promise, however short-lived. His aloofness made him that much more desirable, though she doubted he even realized the power of his mere presence in the room.

Nonetheless, she'd gotten the ball rolling, but would it roll in her favor? That question stuck with her, poking at every nerve in her body as she started the car. She'd done all she could do. Drew's fate might very well rest on Jake Connolly taking the case.

Chapter 7

Andrea opened the door before Lynn had the chance to knock. "I saw you pull in the driveway. Come in."

Lynn walked to the living room doorway and peeked in. Danny was sitting on the couch, glued to the TV. He hadn't seen her yet.

"So," Andrea said, "how did it go?"

"Connolly is going to look into the case. He needs to do some background work first. I think someone wants Drew's disappearance to look like he'd relapsed."

"Why? Why would someone want to do that?"

Lynn shook her head. "I wish I knew."

Andrea looked down at her watch. "Wow. It's almost five. Do you and Danny want to stay for dinner?"

"Thank you, but we need to get home to the puppy." She called out to Danny. "Hey, bud. Get your jacket."

"Aw, Mommy. I'm watching this."

"We're going."

He shuffled to the hall closet, took his jacket off the hook, and wrapped his arms around Andrea's waist. "Bye, Grandma. I love you."

She bent down. "I love you too, sweetheart." She moved her hands up and down his back, then pulled away slightly to kiss his cheek.

As Lynn turned the doorknob, Andrea stopped her. "Lynn." She walked closer. "I...I'm sorry. For everything. You know. Before—"

Lynn put her hand up to stop her. "It's in the past. We're good."

"Still, you didn't deserve the way I treated you. All the things I said. It was just..."

Now she was curious. "Just what?"

"You were the best thing that happened to Drew, such a big part of his recovery, his success." She started to choke up. "When things between the two of you ended, I was upset. Scared mostly that Drew would spiral. I needed someone to blame."

"I get it. For the record though, you're still my favorite mother-in-law."

Andrea laughed. "You're a good person, Lynn." She opened her arms for a hug.

"I'll keep you updated about Drew."

"Race you to the car, Mommy." And off he ran.

"I never walk anymore." She ran to the car.

Once inside and belted in, "Mommy, what's for dinner?"

"Hmm." Lynn tapped her chin. "I'm thinking pizza?"

"Yay. You read my mind."

She chuckled. "Moms do that sometimes." She opened the phone app for Marco's Pizza on Williston Road.

"Mommy, where did you go today?"

She finished typing in the order for a pepperoni and mushroom combo then hit *submit*. "I had to meet with a friend."

Not a complete lie. *If Jake takes the case and finds Drew, I'll be his BFF.*

"Was it about Daddy?"

She couldn't get anything past Danny. There was no point in trying. "Yeah. Since I can't reach Daddy on his phone, I asked for some help."

"So, your friend is going to find him?"

"That's the plan." She plugged her phone into the HandsFreeLink USB port and started the car. "Do you feel like stopping at Aunt Melanie's café while our pizza's being made?"

"Okay." Danny was quiet for about two seconds, then: "I really miss Daddy."

"I know, bud. Me too."

Where are you, Drew?

***

Lynn always loved walking into Melanie's café. The aroma of peanut butter chocolate chip cookies filled the air. A pick-me-up if she ever needed one.

It wasn't just the wonderful smells, though. Everything about Melanie's *Sweets All Around Café* had the power to lift even the lowest of spirits. From the bright colored walls—canary yellow on one end, sea foam green on the other—to the 3-D portraits of heavenly desserts: doughnuts, brownies, eclairs, and coffees that went well with them.

There were strategically placed quotes from famous bakers displayed all around the place. Lynn's favorite was the one above the menu board: "Baking is done out of love, to share with family and friends." —*Anna Olson.*

"Hey, you two," Melanie said from behind the counter. "What a nice surprise."

Lynn followed Danny to the counter where he peered lovingly at all the sweets visible through the glass. "We ordered pizza from Marco's but what's pizza without dessert?"

"A total sin." Melanie laughed.

"I'd like a dozen of your peanut butter chocolate chip cookies."

"Good choice. Fresh out of the oven."

"And a chocolate chip cannoli, too."

"Sure thing." Melanie pulled on a pair of disposable food-service gloves, then reached into the display case. "Did you see a P.I.?" She put Lynn's cookies in a paper bag.

A quick check on Danny told her he was exploring the other end of the counter, cakes and pies, so it was safe to speak freely. "I actually met with one today, Jake Connolly."

"Did he take the case?"

"He's going to look into it. He seems confident, and his success rate is impressive."

"Good. So, he believes you then...that Drew didn't relapse?"

"He wouldn't say, even after I told him I couldn't imagine Drew doing that."

"Me either."

"I'm hoping he takes the case and finds Drew quickly."

Melanie handed her the bag of baked goods. "If you need anything, let me know."

"I might take you up on that."

One of Melanie's employees walked out of the back room, carrying a large tray. "Where should I put this, boss?"

"Over there for now." She pointed to the end of the back counter, across from where Danny was gawking.

Tray delivered, Danny examined the new treats but frowned. "Are those...dog biscuits?"

Melanie laughed. "They sure are." She looked at Lynn. "I'm branching out."

Danny crinkled his eyebrows. "Can I see them closer?"

Melanie walked to the other end of the counter. She took the tray off the back, brought it out front, and placed it on a table so Danny could get a better look. She pointed to the first row of biscuits, which were a light shade of orange. "These are my Sweet Potato Delights with just a pinch of cinnamon sprinkled on top."

"Dogs eat cinnamon?"

"They love it." Melanie smiled. "And it's good for their health." She continued the tour. "Next to those are my Bark-tastic Bacon Biscuits.

Danny laughed.

"And last but not least..." Melanie pointed to the row of red and yellow cookies. "These are my Strawberry and Banana Wafers."

Danny turned wide-eyed to Lynn. "Can we get one for Snowball?"

"Sure. Melanie, how much?"

"You can have one of each, on the house."

"Melanie, are you sure?"

"Snowball will be my official doggy taste-tester."

Danny smiled wide. "Thanks, Aunt Melanie."

"No problem, kiddo." She took the tray back to the counter and placed three biscuits in a blue paper bag with black and white paw prints printed on it. "You'll have to tell me how he likes them. One bark for 'good', two barks and a tail wag for 'great', and three barks with two tail wags for 'woof-underful.'"

He laughed as Melanie handed him the bag. "I bet he's going to woof-love them."

Lynn took him by his free hand. "Come on, bud. Our pizza must be ready by now." She looked at Melanie. "Thanks for everything."

Once they got in the car, Lynn's phone rang from a restricted number. Normally, she wouldn't answer such a call, but under the circumstances, it could be important.

"Hello?"

All she heard was a loud thud, like something heavy hitting concrete. Then the line went dead.

Oh, my God. Drew?

Adrenaline belted her a good one. It had to be a prank call, or a butt-dial...or the sound of a murder...

She was probably over-thinking...but the gut-wrenching worry in her stomach said otherwise.

***

The mysterious call haunted Lynn all through dinner. She put on her best smile when Danny asked about his dad again. They talked about all the fun things he and Drew would do together once he was back home, but inside, she was falling apart with doubt and worry.

Once Danny was tucked in bed, Lynn took her laptop off the desk in her office and walked into the living room, with Snowball following close behind.

He nuzzled at her leg and whimpered.

"Do you want a treat, boy?"

Snowball wagged his tail rapidly.

She walked into the kitchen, dog bouncing at her heels, and retrieved the bag of treats from the counter.

Snowball barked.

"You want one of these?" She reached in and grabbed the Bark-tastic Bacon Biscuit. "How about this one?" Drawing the treat beneath her nose, "Mmmmm," she said to heighten his anticipation.

He barked and stood on his hind legs, a professional beggar pose.

She held the treat up. "Sit."

Snowball sat, tail wagging.

"Good boy." She gave him the treat.

With it clamped in his jaws, he happily followed her back into the living room.

She sat cross-legged on the couch, opened her laptop, and stared at the black screen in front of her, wondering about the success rate of finding missing persons.

Don't look it up. Nothing good can come from it.

Snowball lay on the floor, munching on his bacon treat.

Against her better judgment, she turned the computer on and researched missing persons statistics. The results rattled her. According to the *NamUS* database on missing and unidentified persons, up to 100,000 people are missing at any given time. Along with that, as of 2018, around 11,000 unidentified bodies were housed in coroners' facilities across the country.

Most adult missing persons are those with drug and alcohol addiction, psychiatric problems, and dementia or Alzheimer's patients. Those people are usually found quickly. The ones who remain missing fall within the one percent range.

That's promising.

Drew could be one of the many that are found. But what if he wasn't? What if he stayed missing? Or what if his body was found with no identification?

There was a sudden pain in her chest, then she started to hyperventilate. She lowered her head between her legs until her breathing slowed and the chest pain subsided.

She raised herself up slowly, rested her back against the couch, then tilted her head up to the ceiling.

Help me out here, God. Please. Don't let my son grow up without a father.

Chapter 8

When Monday morning rolled around, Lynn was relieved. She'd spent the entire weekend answering the same questions. 'Where is Daddy?' 'When is he coming home?' 'Did you try calling him again?'

She'd given him the same vaguely optimistic answer every time. 'I'm not sure where he is right now, but I know that he loves you more than anything in the world. And I know he is working super hard to get home.'

It was nice to know that for the next six hours she'd be question free, until Danny came home from school.

"Have a good day, honey," she said when the school bus arrived. She went to give him a hug and kiss, but he quickly pulled away when he saw his friends looking at him through the windows.

"Bye," he called out as he jetted to the bus.

She could see Danny waving to someone, a little girl with frizzy blond hair and brown eyes. She was smiling and waving back to him. She must have been

Lexie Turner, the girl Danny had been talking about for the past few months. 'Lexie showed me the coolest trick on the playground.' 'Lexie draws the best dinosaurs.' 'Lexie said she wants to be an artist when she grows up.'

Lynn watched the bus leave, then headed into the house to get ready for work. She quickly threw on a blue collard blouse and beige khaki pants then hurried into the kitchen and grabbed her purse and keys off the table, feeling anxious to get to her office.

She was meeting with Violet Miller at eleven to discuss the details of her mother's birthday party.

With Drew missing, she needed a good distraction. Hopefully, this time, her meeting with Violet would go off without a hitch.

***

On her way to work, the HandsFreeLink phone system buzzed in a call from a number she didn't recognize on the dash display. Hoping it was Drew, she pressed the 'talk' button on the steering wheel. "Hello?"

"Good morning, Ms. Callahan. This is Officer Diaz. We met last week."

"Officer?" Her stomach started jumping.

"I need you to come down to the station this morning."

"I'm on my way to work, but I can be late."

"I'll let the front desk know to expect you."

"Wait. Officer Diaz. Why? Should I be worried? Is it about Drew? Did you find him? Is—is he okay?" Her voice cracked with panic.

"We have new information regarding the case. I'll explain everything when you get here."

She sighed. "On my way."

She re-routed her car in the direction of the police station while trying to remain calm and rational. According to Officer Diaz's persistence, there must be a break in the case. Why else would he be calling?

The phone chimed in another call. *Connolly Investigations* came up on the dash display. Her heart started to pound. "Mr. Connolly. What have you learned?"

"Morning, Ms. Callahan. I've done some preliminary interviews and believe something is fishy about your ex-husband's disappearance."

"Does that mean you'll take the case?"

"You'll need to come by the office so we can discuss the terms of the contract. This afternoon be okay?"

"Yes, after Danny gets home from school, let's say 4:00?"

"See you then."

"Thank you. Thank you. Thank you."

He hung up.

She did a happy dance in her seat.

We're going to find you, Drew.

***

It took seven minutes for her to get to the police station. When she walked through the glass doors, she felt a dire sense of urgency as she saw officers, none of them smiling, scramble across the lobby with purpose in their steps. Each had the weight of the world on their shoulders. She heard phones ringing and unintelligible radio chatter and wondered who else was calling for help. Realizing this bustle went on day after day overwhelmed her with uncertainty. Her problem with Drew was just a ripple in a raging river.

A loud commotion made her turn to see an officer enter the station, escorting a man with his hands cuffed behind him. He shouted slurred obscenities at anyone near him. She stepped back to get out of the way, but he scowled and lunged at her. "What are you looking at, bitch?" The putrid smell of vomit and alcohol rolled from his breath and slugged her in the face.

"That's enough," the officer said. "Come on." He yanked the man away from her.

When they left through a back door, she looked down to make sure she hadn't peed in her pants, then made her way to the front desk. "I'm Lynn Callahan," she said to the duty officer. "I'm here to see Officer Diaz. He called and asked me to come down."

"Right. Ms. Callahan. I'll let him know you're here."

Moments later, she saw Officer Diaz fast-stepping toward her. He was carrying a manilla folder. "Ms. Callahan, thank for coming down." He extended his free hand.

She accepted his handshake. "Officer Diaz, respectfully, I'm scared out of my mind. I need to know. Did you find Drew?"

"Follow me." He led her down a long hallway, then stopped in front of a door and opened it. "After you."

The room was bright and crammed with file cabinets and bookcases.

"Have a seat." He pointed to a chair behind a dark conference table then sat cattywampus to her.

"Officer Diaz, I'm not trying to be impatient, but why am I here?"

He set the folder on the table. "Your ex-husband's car was found in the parking lot of Essex Junction Station."

She frowned and tugged nervously on the collar of her blouse. "The Amtrak Depot?"

"I called you in so you can see the evidence for yourself." He opened the manilla folder and took out a picture of the car as the police had found it.

There was no mistake. It had Drew's license plate and a small dent on the rear quarter-panel where Danny had crashed his bike into it.

"A one-way ticket to New York was purchased with his credit card."

"There must be an explanation. I told you. Drew would never leave Danny. Someone must have taken Drew and used his credit card."

"Ms. Callahan. There's no evidence anyone kidnapped him. Face it. Everything points to him not wanting to be found. Happens all the time."

"But you don't know Drew the way I do."

"I'm sorry, ma'am. I've notified the NYPD and sent them a BOLO.

"Be on the lookout? He's not a criminal."

"The investigation is in their hands now."

Oh, how wrong you are.

Chapter 9

Violet arrived five minutes before her scheduled appointment. She was smiling when she entered Lynn's office. "I hope we don't get interrupted this time." Her red high heels clacked against the floor as she walked toward the chair opposite Lynn's desk.

"How was your weekend?"

She flattened out her white sundress. "Relaxing. And yours?"

"The same," Lynn lied. "Okay, let's get down to business." She took a notebook out from her middle desk drawer and readied a pen. "You're looking at two months from now, right?"

Violet nodded. "June 21st."

Lynn made a note. "How many guests?"

"Fifty."

"Your mother has a lot of friends. Do you have a venue in mind?"

"Cucina Cappitani, her favorite restaurant."

"They have a nice party room with a band stage, and they can easily accommodate fifty." Lynn wrote down the name. "I like to have a couple of backup venues, in case the date is unavailable. I recommend the Community Sailing Center and Arrowhead Golf Course if I can't get Cucina Cappitani—"

"I've already booked the date with them."

"That helps. Regarding food, any specific requests I can have the restaurant prepare?"

"They have the best Italian. For appetizers, I'm thinking bruschetta, stuffed mushrooms, and garlic knots. And for the entrees, chicken picatta, penne alla vodka, and eggplant parmesan. All her favorites."

Lynn smiled. "A woman after my own heart. Now, for dessert, I get a lot of requests for chocolate fudge cake. What do you think?"

"My mom's a fan of anything chocolate, but she especially loves chocolate eclairs."

"Perfect. I know just the place to get them."

"I'd also like something special for entertainment. Can we get a Billy Joel tribute band?"

"Love it, but our regular band quit, so I'll start calling local bands. We can audition them together."

"My mom will really appreciate that."

By the end of their meeting, Lynn felt like she knew Violet Miller's mother. Her favorite color was blue, her favorite flowers were lilies, and she loved Billy Joel. "Alright, Violet, I have all the information I need. See the front desk for payment options."

She stood from her chair, all smiles. "It's going to be a great party."

A few hours after Violet left, Lynn's phone rang. It was Jake.

"Something's come up. Can you come to my office earlier? Say 2:45?"

She glanced up at her wall clock. *2:15*. A drive across town would make her late for when Danny got home from school. She'd need to meet Jake somewhere closer to home. "How about we meet at The Silver Spoon Café so I can be home when my son gets off the school bus?"

"Silver Spoon...I can do that. See you there."

As Lynn was getting ready to leave her office, she started to wonder what Jake had learned that convinced him to take the case. Was Dale involved in his disappearance? Was it someone else from his past? Or was Jake right about Drew's ex, Theresa? She had just as many questions for Jake as Danny had for her.

***

Lynn had been to the Silver Spoon Café a few times over the years. It was a nice, homey place, only a few blocks from her house. The food was good, the servers were friendly, and it was never overcrowded, but the sweets didn't hold a candle to Melanie's café.

Jake was already there, sitting at a corner table, next to the coffee shop's entrance. He had set a satchel on the chair beside him.

Lynn sat across from him. "Thanks for agreeing to meet here." She placed her purse on the table and pushed it toward the window.

"I took the liberty of ordering you a coffee though I'm not sure how you like it, so I got it black, with cream and sugar on the side."

"Coffee is just what I need." She tore a sugar packet open and poured it in with the cream, then mixed it together with a silver spoon.

He slid an official-looking document toward her. "Let's get this paperwork out of the way."

She sipped coffee then gave it a quick once-over. The contract.

"I charge one hundred dollars an hour plus expenses, due on completion of my investigation. I'll need a five-hundred-dollar retainer." He held out a pen.

"What if you don't find Drew?"

"No guarantees." He wagged the pen.

"That's fine. I have faith in your reputation." She took the pen, signed the contract, and slid it back to him.

"I accept cash and checks. No credit cards."

She opened her purse and removed a checkbook. "Five hundred, you say? What if you find him in two hours?"

"Good for you." He said it with a sly smile.

His confidence was rather appealing. She wrote the check and slid it to him. "I'd like to know what made you decide to take the case."

He dropped the contract and check into his satchel and removed a notebook. "You were right about Drew's ex-girlfriend, Theresa Lambert."

"Oh?"

"She called Drew two weeks ago, but they haven't talked since then. She has a solid alibi for the day Drew went missing. I don't believe she had anything to do with this."

"That's good, I guess. Narrowing down the suspect pool. Did she say why she called him?"

"No, and I didn't ask. Doesn't matter, really. I also spoke with Drew's current girlfriend, Beth Meyers. They've been dating for two months. The last time she saw him was last week, two days before he went missing."

"Where was she at the time?"

"She worked from nine to five on Friday. I also checked her alibi for Thursday night since that was the last time Charlie said he'd spoken with Drew. Beth went to a ten o'clock movie with a few friends at Essex Cinemas. The theater confirmed their ticket purchases."

"So, Beth is in the clear then."

"She hasn't given me a reason not to believe her, but my staff is running a background check on her."

"That's all fine and dandy, but what got you hooked on this case?"

"What his neighbor had to say...at his apartment building. If the police had taken this case more seriously, they'd have been intrigued, as well."

Lynn exhaled sharply. "They doubted there was any foul play."

Jake shook his finger and smiled a little. "One of Drew's neighbors said she heard an argument coming from his apartment late Thursday night. She went over there to tell them to knock it off, but when she got to his door, the arguing had stopped."

"Arguing about what?"

"She couldn't make out the words, but clearly it was loud."

"So...Drew wasn't alone."

"Here's where it gets interesting. Sometime after midnight, she heard shuffling in the hallway. By the time she looked out her door, the elevator was closing, but she swore she saw two men inside. A few minutes later, she heard two cars start up. She looked out her window and saw them racing out of the lot. She didn't know the make and model of the cars, and it was too dark to make out their colors. I checked traffic cam footage around that area and saw Drew's car. Two people were in it. The passenger's head was tilted down, and the driver wore a hat and sunglasses. The car behind Drew's car was a tan Honda sedan, no plates, but it had a University of Vermont sticker on the front bumper. The driver wore a surgical mask."

"That's not much to go on, could be anyone, a current student or an alum."

"But it's a start."

"Drew may have been knocked out, you think?"

"It's hard to tell."

"Do you think Dale was driving Drew's car?"

"With that thought in mind, I went to interview him, but sadly, his family told me that five months ago, Dale took a fistful of pills and crashed his car into a tree. He's been in a coma ever since. The official report stated a suicide attempt."

"That eliminates him as a suspect. But...but maybe a relative blames Drew for Dale's predicament."

"I don't want to jump to conclusions, but I'm intrigued enough to take your case."

"It is a puzzle, isn't it."

"I'm going to do some digging into Dale's life, see who was closest to him and get their stories."

"Okay. Yeah." She held her hands together, tightly. "It's just...the not knowing."

"Hey, look at me." His words were soft, his tone sympathetic. "I think *you're* the puzzle here."

"Me?"

"You still love him, don't you."

"He's my son's father."

He leaned forward and stretched his arms across the table. His fingers interlaced with hers. "I'm going to get to the bottom of this."

She found his light touch to be warm and comforting. "I needed to hear that. Thanks."

"You're welcome." Jake held her gaze then pulled back. "I'm going to the university tomorrow morning to speak with Drew's co-workers and students. Maybe they saw or heard something that can shed light on his disappearance."

"Be sure to talk to Charlie Benson." She took her purse off the table, then pushed her chair back and stood. "Thank you for taking the case."

He stood and dropped a twenty on the table. "I'll keep you updated with what I find."

"Oh...by the way, there's something I found out

that you should know. I talked with Officer Diaz. Drew's car was found at the train station. A one-way ticket to New York City was put on his credit card."

"Hmmm. But did Drew board the train?"

"As crazy as it may sound, I doubt it. He wouldn't leave his son stranded at school. They had a whole weekend planned together."

"Let me walk you out." Jake held the door open and ushered Lynn outside. "Where are you parked?"

"Over there." She pointed straight ahead to her white Pilot in the parking lot.

"I'll walk you over."

She smiled. "Quite the gentleman. How much will it cost me?"

"Not to worry. I'm off the clock."

She laughed, and not paying attention to where she stepped, her right high-heel caught a crack in the pavement. She went down like a rock. Her purse went flying, and her right elbow took the brunt of the fall. She lay there, mortified by her clumsy move, and groaned while taking mental inventory for broken bones.

Jake knelt beside her. "My God, girl. Are you okay?"

"Yeah. Just a little embarrassed."

He helped her sit up, examined her elbow.

"That's going to need a bandage."

"I'm such a klutz."

"Sometimes gravity can be a nuisance." He wrapped one arm around her waist and lifted her off the ground like she weighed nothing.

Strangers gathered around. "Are you alright?" "What happened?" "Should I call 911?"

"I got this, everyone." He set her on her feet. "Can you walk?"

"I think so." But the moment she put pressure on her right ankle, she stumbled. Jake caught her, held her upright. With her entire right side pressed against his hard body, she nearly lost the ability to breathe, and out of nowhere, she wondered what muscles his button-down shirt was concealing. She shook her head to dispel her wild imagination. "I think I sprained it."

He picked up her purse and the satchel he'd dropped. "That's it. I'm driving you home." He carried her the few steps to her car. "I'll come back for my car later."

She sighed lightly. "I don't want to be a bother."

What am I thinking? Of course I want to be a bother. He's cute, yes. Okay, no, he's hot. But I need to be home when Danny gets off the bus, and I need to focus on finding Drew.

Chapter 10

When Jake carried Lynn through her front door, Snowball came barreling down the hall, barking and growling at Jake. As small as he was, Snowball was extremely protective.

"Hey, there, buddy." He lowered Lynn to a standing position, then he bent down and placed his hand out for Snowball to sniff. "You're a good dog."

Snowball approached Jake cautiously. He sniffed around his hand then licked Jake's fingers and began wagging his tail.

"Okay, we're good." He stood. "As for you, young lady, let me get you off your feet." After helping her walk into the living room, he laid her on the couch. "You should rest that ankle." He propped her leg up with a couple of throw pillows.

Snowball was quick to follow. He whimpered a little, as if he could tell Lynn wasn't her cheerful self. Jake lifted the dog up and placed him in the crook of Lynn's arm.

"Since you're in good hands, I'll go get you an icepack for your ankle."

"The kitchen's just down the hall."

He came back a few minutes later with a plastic bag of ice wrapped in a paper towel. "I just want to take a look, before I put the ice on it."

"Be careful. It hurts like hell." She stroked Snowball's fur.

He lifted her pantleg. "It's a little swollen, but I think you'll live." He set the makeshift icepack on her ankle.

"I know I said it before but thank you."

"I couldn't just leave you in the parking lot with a bum ankle."

Lynn laughed a little. "If you were on the clock, I'd have run you off."

"Do you need anything else before I head out? Water maybe?"

"You can hand me the remote." She motioned to the center of the coffee table.

He handed her the remote. "We'll talk soon."

As he was heading toward the door, she called out to him. "Wait. I forgot to tell you something."

He turned and walked back to her. "What is it?"

"On Saturday night, I got a strange call from a restricted number. When I answered, there was no response, just a loud thud before the line went dead."

"You think it was Drew trying to reach out?"

"It sounded like a body landing on cement."

"I'll check your phone records, see if I can find the number that called you. Good work, detective." He chuckled, opened his mouth, and then closed it quickly, as if he wanted to say something he shouldn't.

Her interest peaked. "What?" She tilted her head to the side.

"Nothing. I should go. Take it easy on that ankle." He started to walk away.

She grabbed his hand and pulled him back toward her. "Sit down. Please."

"Okay..." He claimed the accent chair across from the couch. "What's on your mind?"

"You wanted to say something. Why did you stop yourself?"

"Oh, that. I was curious about something..."

"Just ask."

He exhaled slowly, then: "I've been hired by wives before, husbands too. They usually want dirt on each other. It can get brutal, but this case...you, you seem to really care about your ex. I'm just curious why you got divorced?"

She sighed. "Drew's addiction took its toll. Over time, we grew apart. There was no spark left, snuffed out by all the drama. Other than Danny, we no longer had anything in common."

"Yeah. Addiction has a way of doing that to people. Thanks for clearing that up."

"Now I have a question for you."

"That's fair. Shoot."

"Before I hired you, I did my research. I know you got shot on the job while chasing a suspect, but it seems to me that you made a full recovery, and you're clearly a talented detective. So, why did you leave the force?"

"It's true, physically I could have gone back, but mentally and emotionally, I was hogtied."

"What happened the day you got shot?"

"My partner, Detective Trent Martin...my partner and I were investigating the murder of a college student. She was the fourth victim of the same killer in nearly six months. We went a few weeks without any viable leads, until finally we had a suspect who had means, motive, and opportunity. We were able to get his location. He was at a seafood restaurant, sitting at a table, eating his shrimp scampi, like nothing bothered him." Jake looked down at the floor.

"Oh. I'm sorry. You don't have to talk about it."

He looked up. "I'm okay. The suspect saw us the minute we walked in and drew his gun. He shot my partner, and I made the mistake of looking down at my friend, and in that second, the suspect shot me.

The bullet blew out my left lung, but I got off two shots as I went down. Got the bastard twice in the chest, but that small victory came at a high price."

She was at a loss for words. "I can't imagine..."

"I replayed that moment over and over in my head, wondering if I could have done something different, to make sure Trent went home to his family instead of to the morgue in a body bag." He exhaled deeply, his hand shaking a little.

"You don't have to continue."

"The more I tell this story the easier it becomes to accept my failures." He placed his hand on his leg. "After my recovery, I was set to return to work, but the minute I stepped foot in that precinct, I saw Trent, eyes wide open on the floor of the restaurant. I saw his wife fall to her knees when I told her what happened, and I heard the cries of their newborn baby. That's when I knew I would be of little use to a new partner."

"Your P.I. business takes less of an emotional toll?"

"I can investigate mysteries, get justice, of sorts, but it's not as dangerous. And I set my own hours."

"That's always a plus."

"Yeah. But even now there are days when I can't get out of bed."

Katelyn Marie Peterson

"Are you sure it's not PTSD?"

"It's something, alright. If it were up to my mom, though, I'd have a safer job, like my siblings. My brother is a motivational speaker, and my sister is an athletic trainer."

"Your family never wanted you to be a cop?"

He shook his head. "Mom tried to talk me out of it a few times, but eventually she came to terms with my decision. She said she was proud of me, but I could tell she was scared, the way she'd hug me so tight whenever I left her, as if it would be the last time she'd see me."

"As a mom, I get it. We want our kids to be safe, always. Sometimes I wish I could put Danny in a bubble, away from all the bad in the world."

"Until the bubble pops." His expression turned solemn. "It always pops."

"I can't speak for your mom, but I will always be proud of Danny, even if his choices terrify me. What about your dad? Did he try to talk you out of it, too?"

"My parents got divorced when I was eleven. My mom moved to Vermont with us kids, and my dad stayed in Ohio. He never tried to be a part of our lives. We got Christmas and birthday cards and the occasional phone call, but the conversations never lasted more than a few minutes. When I told him

~84~

about my decision to become a cop, he simply said, 'Don't get shot.'"

"Wow. How did he react when you actually did get shot?"

"I never told him. If he found out, he never said anything."

"That must be hard. I can't imagine going that long without talking to my dad."

"It was hard when I was a kid, but after a while I realized I needed to appreciate the parent who was there, rather than resent the one who wasn't."

Silence fell between them. She knew they had both shared key pieces of themselves, personal and painful. Why? Why was it so easy for her to talk to this man, someone she barely knew, yet felt so comfortable with? The phenomenon would have unnerved her if she weren't so attracted to him.

The school bus screeched to a stop in front of the house. Jake stood. "I think that's my cue to go."

"You don't have to rush off." She placed Snowball on the floor, then slowly swung her legs off the couch. "I'll drive you to your car. Danny can come with us."

"I'll catch an Uber. You stay put."

Danny ran up the front steps and paused to watch Jake walk off with a cell phone to his ear. "Who was that, Mommy?"

"Hey, bud." She'd gotten up from the couch and walked to the doorway. Her ankle was still sore, but icing it had eased the pain. "How was school?"

"Fine." Danny kept his eyes on Jake as he stood at the curb. "Mommy?" He turned to face her. "Does that man know Daddy?"

Snowball was bouncing around Danny, all doggy happy to see him.

"That's the friend I was telling you about."

"Oh, the one who's looking for Daddy?"

"Yeah, that friend."

"Did you tell him to hurry?"

"He knows, honey. He knows."

And that was that. Dog and boy ran off to play.

For the first time since Drew went missing, she truly believed he would be found, and that Jake was going to bring him home and end her nightmare.

But the question remained. Would Drew be found alive?

Chapter 11

L ynn spent most of the next day on pins and needles, waiting to hear from Jake about his meeting with Drew's co-workers. Her heart jumped every time her phone rang or chimed with a text.

She tried to keep calm by repeating the words "no news is good news." *What a load of crap.* She stared intently at her quiet phone, as if she had the power to make it ring with good news.

If only.

She knew she had no control over Jake's investigation or its outcome, but it was hard to accept. As an event planner, having control was essential. And as a mother, if she didn't have control...well, home life would be chaos.

Do what you know.

Lynn pushed all thoughts of Drew and Jake out of her mind. Instead, she focused all her energy on planning the best birthday party for Violet Miller's mother, Lydia.

She started with the venue. She called Cucina

Cappitani to confirm that they booked the date, then having Violet's preferred menu, she conferred with the head cook to prepare all of Lydia Miller's favorite foods: bruschetta, stuffed mushrooms, and garlic knots for appetizers; chicken picatta, penne alla vodka, and eggplant parmesan for the entrees.

She dropped Melanie's name when they were talking about dessert. "I'll use *Sweets All Around Café*. Their desserts are always a big hit with the guests."

Violet e-mailed her several pictures of Lydia and asked for a custom poster. The idea was to have a current photo of Lydia in the center, surrounded by smaller pictures from her childhood. Above the photos, the poster would read, 'Sixty Years Young.'

After making a couple more calls and sending a few e-mails, Lynn leaned back and let out a relieved sigh. She'd accomplished everything she needed to for Lydia's birthday party, aside from the flowers, the band auditions, and the final set-up map for the party room.

She wished everything in life could be that simple, but in the same breath she knew that planning a birthday party wasn't nearly as exciting as finding clues and chasing down leads in the search for Drew.

***

While she was driving home from work, her

phone rang. It was Jake.

Finally.

"How did it go at the university?"

"Let me start off by saying that you were right about Drew not going to New York." His smooth voice came over the HandsFreeLink speakers. "I checked the train station's video footage from Thursday night and Friday morning. There was no sign of Drew boarding the train."

"I told the cops that Drew didn't leave Danny." She stopped the car for a red light.

"The parking lot footage showed someone stepping out of Drew's car Friday morning, around 12:30 A.M. That person left the train station on foot."

"But not Drew, right?"

"No. This person was shorter. He was wearing a hoodie and kept his head low. His right hand was at his ear, as if he was talking on a cell phone."

"At least we know Drew's car was a red herring."

"Yeah. Somebody is up to no good."

"What did you find at the university?"

"I spoke with Drew's colleagues. It turns out there was a confrontation recently between him and one of his students. A guy named Ray Jackson."

"What happened?" She merged the car into the flow of traffic on Main.

Jake scoffed. "Ray was unhappy with a grade he'd gotten on an assignment, made a big scene in class. And get this, some of Drew's other students said that Ray is known for being a mule for a notorious campus drug dealer."

Lynn's eyes widened. "The pill bottles in Drew's apartment. Could Ray have put them there to throw off any investigation?"

"It's possible. Remember how the traffic cam footage showed a Honda sedan with a University of Vermont bumper sticker? Ray has a car just like it."

Lynn gasped. "That's great, right? That means you can tie Ray to Drew's disappearance."

"Not quite. The license plates were missing. Could be one of thousands of Honda's registered in this county. However, I took a shot and spoke with Ray. He claimed to be in his dorm room Thursday night, playing video games with his roommate, David Lane, and he was in class Friday morning, waiting for the professor to show up."

"And you're sure he was there?"

"I confirmed both alibis, but something with the roommate was off. He didn't look me in the eyes when I asked him if he was with Ray Thursday night, and he spoke with quick, concise words, like he'd rehearsed the lines. I'll give him a little time to sweat then interrogate him again. I'm not done with David Lane."

She gripped her steering wheel, her knuckles turning white. "You think Ray kidnapped Drew and stole his car because of a stupid grade?"

"I'm not sure about that. Ray may have a grudge against Drew, but he doesn't strike me as the type who's smart enough to pull off a kidnapping. I do believe he can be easily manipulated by someone with their own grudge."

"What does that mean?"

He cleared his throat. "Lynn, did you know that Drew's friend Charlie Benson was fired last Monday?"

"He what? No. When we spoke on the phone, he said he saw Drew at work on Thursday."

"He lied. He was barred from the campus. Apparently, Mr. Benson has had quite the temper lately. The week before, he'd flipped over a desk during one of his classes. That's what got him fired."

"I can't believe he lied to me...but I'm...I'm confused. What does any of that have to do with Drew?"

Jake sighed. "Drew is the one who alerted the university to Mr. Benson's bad behavior."

Her heart lurched. "Please tell me Charlie doesn't

know that."

"The university didn't name Drew, but Charlie put two-and-two together. He completely lost it. He said Drew was an unreliable source, claiming that his past wasn't so much in the past anymore."

"Are you serious?"

"He told them Drew was back to using drugs. They didn't believe him for a second, but according to university policy, they had to order Drew to take a drug test."

"They've known each other for a decade. I can't believe Charlie would betray Drew like that." Everything around her became a blur. All she could focus on was her anger, until the driver in the lane next to her slammed on his horn. Her car had started to drift out of her lane. She swerved and refocused on the road, gripped the steering wheel tighter, and took a deep breath.

"The good news," Jake said, "is that Drew passed the drug test. Now we have concrete proof that he's clean."

She banged her fist on the steering wheel. "I knew it. So, you believe Charlie is responsible for Drew's disappearance?"

"It's a solid theory. He has motive and means, and he's five-foot-seven, so he could have been the perp on the train station's parking lot footage."

"Maybe he was on his way to meet up with Ray."

"Problem is, I'm not sure if Charlie had the opportunity. He claims to have been at The Whiskey Room Thursday night and stayed there 'til closing when he left with a woman, claimed he was with her all of Friday morning."

Lynn scoffed. "I wonder what his wife would say about that."

"I'm going to check his alibi. All we know right now is that Drew's disappearance looks to have been a two-person job. One takes him for a ride in his car, the other steals his wallet and credit cards."

"But someone has to be the brains of the bunch." She put her left turn signal on. "What about the Dale Hogan angle...that a family member was out for revenge against Drew?"

"His parents have solid alibis. His sister lives in Florida. The last time she spoke to Dale was a few months before the car crash. She suspected that he was using again because he'd stopped going to his rehab meetings. Dale told her he was clean and didn't need them anymore. He apologized for the hell he'd put the family through. It was part of his atonement to make amends for his addiction. When she heard that he was in a coma, she started visiting him every other month."

"So, she had motive to go after Drew."

"It doesn't look that way. She didn't know Drew had rebuffed Dale, and he was in no condition to tell her. Besides, she's got a good job, two kids, and a busy social life. I doubt she had anything to do with it. Plus, she and her husband were on vacation all last week."

"So, we're back to Charlie." She groaned. "What if his alibi checks out? What then?" She slammed on her brakes, nearly running over a clown on a bicycle. A glance at her mirror told her no one was behind her.

"Then I'll dive deeper into Dale's life. His sister gave me the names of three of his friends. I'll dig into their social lives, see if there's any connection, even the tiniest, to Ray Jackson or David Lane. And if that doesn't pan out, Ray will be my focus. Maybe he's smarter than I thought."

"What are we, dogs chasing our tails?" She didn't hide the doubt and despair in her voice. "This investigation is turning into a game of Whack-a-Mole."

"Lynn, do you still trust me?"

"I don't doubt your skills as a P.I., if that's what you're asking, but it seems whoever is responsible for Drew's disappearance is good at covering their tracks."

"And I'm good at finding clues. I will not stop until I've investigated every single one of them."

"It's just frustrating..." She turned onto her street, grateful that she was almost home, away from moving cars.

"We'll talk soon. Oh, I almost forgot. I ran the background check on Beth Meyers. She got a couple of speeding tickets last year, but other than that, she's clean."

"Another dead end, of course."

"Keep the faith." He hung up.

Don't lose hope. Remember, Jake knows what he's doing.

Chapter 12

When Lynn arrived at home, she was surprised to see Andrea's car parked out front. She was pacing across the front porch.

Lynn got out of the car. "Andrea? Is something wrong?"

"I'm sorry for just showing up like this. I know I should have called first."

"You don't have to apologize. Are you alright?"

"Yeah. Yeah. I umm...I just wanted to see how things are going with the investigation."

She could see that Andrea wasn't alright. She had dark circles under her eyes and the color was drained from her face. Lynn wondered if Andrea had gotten any sleep or if she'd eaten lately. "Come on inside." She unlocked the front door.

Seated on the couch with Andrea, and before Lynn had the chance to say anything, Snowball bounded into the living room and started barking at Andrea like he had done with Jake.

"Well, hello there," Andrea said. "Aren't you a

cutie?"

Snowball stopped barking and licked her extended hand as if he knew that she needed cheering up.

She patted Snowball gently on the head, then picked him up and placed him in her lap. "What a good boy...boy? Right?"

"Yes. Snowball." Lynn tilted her head. "The investigation is ongoing. I just spoke with the P.I. He has a couple of leads, nothing solid yet."

Andrea's eyes drooped. "I-I just want Drew found." Her chin quivered.

Lynn reached for Andrea's hand. "Me too. I was going to call you as soon as I got home."

"I had to come see you...I feel so alone." She placed Snowball on the floor.

"This is hard. For everyone."

Andrea stood. "In any case, I better go." She started for the door.

"Wait. No need to rush off. You just got here." Lynn stopped her with a gentle hand to the shoulder. "Danny will be home any minute. You're welcome to stay for dinner."

She turned, now teary-eyed. "A family dinner would be good for me."

"Me too."

Danny bounded in through the door. "Grandma. Grandma." He threw his arms around her. "You're here. You're here."

"And she's staying for dinner."

"Yay."

Snowball was jumping around them.

Lynn's heart felt warm as she watched a tattered family come together in the midst of a baffling mystery. In the kitchen, she opened the refrigerator to retrieve a package of ground beef. It was Taco Tuesday in the Callahan house.

As she was preparing the meat, Lynn could hear Danny talking to Andrea in the living room. He was telling her a joke he'd heard at school. His infectious laugh at the punchline spread to Andrea.

"Oh, honey, you are just what the doctor ordered," she said, while trying to catch her breath.

There was a moment of silence, then Danny said, "Why, Grandma? Are you sick?"

"Oh, no. I'm perfectly fine. It's just an expression. It means that you make me happy."

"Oh. That's good."

As Lynn was dishing the ground beef into a serving bowl, Snowball came over and snuggled her leg then gave a gentle bark.

"I haven't forgotten about you. Your food is

coming up." She carried the serving bowl and three plates to the table, then walked to the pantry for Snowball's food. After filling his dog dish, she set it on the floor. "There you go, boy."

Snowball chowed down.

She walked to the oven, took out a pan of warm taco shells, and placed it on the kitchen table. Then she headed back for the toppings: lettuce, tomatoes, cheese, and sour cream. "Dinner is ready."

Once they were seated, "I can't remember the last time I had tacos," Andrea said while filling a taco shell to the brim.

Danny looked at her wide-eyed. "Really? We have them every week." He was a pro at stuffing his taco.

"Lucky you." Andrea took a bite of her masterpiece.

"Mommy, when Daddy comes back, maybe he and Grandma can come have tacos with us a lot."

Danny was a fun and hopeful kid. He was always telling jokes, making up stories, and talking excitedly about the future.

Lynn looked at Andrea and saw her eyes well with tears, spurring her own emotional bucket to spring a leak.

Danny looked from Lynn to Andrea and gave

them a puzzled scowl. "Did I say something wrong?"

"Not at all, bud."

Andrea chimed in. "We would love to join you for tacos."

Good job, Andrea.

After dinner and a couple of T.V. shows, Lynn said, "Time for bed, bud."

"Can't I stay up a little longer?"

"Sorry, kiddo. You have school tomorrow."

Andrea laughed. "And your grandma needs to go to bed too." She got up from her chair. "Can I have a hug?"

"Uh-huh." Danny gave her a big squeeze. "Bye, Grandma."

"Bye, sweetheart."

Lynn walked Andrea to the door.

"I feel like I've been saying this a lot lately, but again, thank you for including me in your Taco Tuesday. I feel like I've got a family now, somewhere I truly belong, and I had a great time."

"Me too." She gave Andrea a hug. "Drive safe."

Lynn closed the door, then turned to Danny. "Come on. Let's get you to bed." She indicated the stairs with her index finger.

Danny slumped his shoulders. "I never get to stay up late."

Once he was tucked into bed, Lynn retreated to the living room, plopped herself onto the couch, and surfed the channels until she found a sitcom to watch. Soon, the canned laughter faded, voices dimmed, and the doorbell rang, strange in the way it echoed around her. She opened her eyes to see Jake standing above her.

"Hey, beautiful." He wore blue jeans and a tight-fitting white t-shirt. His chiseled chest would make Adonis jealous.

She stood up from the couch and edged away. "You shouldn't be here," she said softly. "Danny is asleep."

He stepped in closer. "Do you want me to leave?"

She basked in the muskiness of his cologne, an aphrodisiac she realized as butterflies fluttered in places down low. "I want you to make love to me." She couldn't believe the words that came out of her mouth.

The shock on his face faded in and out. He cupped her chin in his hand and stroked her cheek gently with his thumb. "I haven't stopped thinking about you."

His gentle touch sent a wave of warmth through her belly. "I've been thinking about you too," she whispered.

He moved his hand from her cheek down to her waist and pulled her body into his. While removing her shirt and bra, his seductive eyes never left her. She moved her hands up and down his chest, then lifted his shirt up over his head. The feeling of her bare breasts against his bare chest caused her entire body to tighten. "Oh, Jake." She looped her arms around his neck and went in for a kiss. Finally to taste those soft lips...

He gently held her back. "I found Drew."

Her eyes flew open, and she gasped. "What?" She looked around her living room, the air filled with canned laughter and the flicker of the television. No bare-chested Jake. No musky cologne. She was fully dressed, but the butterflies persisted.

She sat up, breathless, and never felt more alone.

What's wrong with me? He's only in my life to find Drew.

She wasn't delusional. Jake would be gone soon enough, but in her fantasy world, once Drew was found, Jake would sweep her up in his arms and bring her dream to life.

If only that were true.

Chapter 13

The next morning, Lynn woke up to the sound of Danny screaming. "Mommy. Mommy." His frantic footsteps raced down the hallway.

She shot out of bed and met him at the door. "What's the matter?"

"Daddy's dead," he shouted through panicked sobs.

She bent down and scooped him into her arms. "No, honey." She stroked the back of his head. "Daddy isn't dead."

"He is. I saw him. He was on the ground and not moving."

"It was just a bad dream. It wasn't real, honey. Come on, let's sit." She took Danny by the hand and walked him to the foot of her bed where they sat together in a mom-and-son hug.

"Are you sure he's not dead?" He looked at her while tears ran down his cheeks.

"I'm sure your dream was scary." She had to get him to think about something else to keep the lingering nightmare at bay. "Listen, how would you like to stay home today?"

"You mean...I don't have to go to school?"

"Nope."

"But what about Lexie...and my friends?"

"You'll see them tomorrow."

He wiped away tears with his hand. "Can we go to the park?"

"You bet, but first, let's eat."

Though dawn was an hour from breaking, Lynn fixed a simple breakfast: cereal and a bowl of fruit.

He dug in and crunched Coco Puffs. "Can we take Snowball with us?"

"Of course we can."

"Yay." Danny waved his spoon excitedly.

"Easy, bud." She laughed.

It was nice to see Danny smile after the night terrors he'd suffered. Since Drew went missing, she spent half of her time trying to reassure Danny that his dad was coming home, and the other half trying to distract him from Drew altogether.

When they finished breakfast, she walked to the hall closet and took down a backpack from the top shelf. She filled it with the contents from her purse, along with two water bottles and a zip-lock bag of snacks.

"Are we going for a hike?" Danny asked.

"You'll see. We need to get dressed first. She helped him pick an outfit befitting the spring weather: green khaki pants and a yellow t-shirt with a big green dinosaur on it.

Once he was ready, Lynn rushed to her bedroom and pulled on a pair of black jogger pants and a pink workout-T.

When she got to the front door, Danny was waiting for her with Snowball in his arms. "Don't forget the backpack, Mommy." He looked down at the bag leaning beside the front door.

"Thanks, bud." She picked up the bag then followed him out the door, running, of course.

Commence operation *Keep Danny Happy*.

***

Lynn pulled her car into a space for Ethan Allen Park, one of Danny's favorite places in the world. "Okay, bud. We're here."

He smiled wide and looked down at Snowball. "We're here, boy." His voice screeched with excitement.

Lynn watched as Danny ran ahead of her toward the playground with Snowball running beside him. "Danny, be careful. Slow down." She pictured the two of them crashing into each other and getting twisted up in Snowball's leash.

"I want to do the slide first." He looked down at Snowball who was wagging his tail excitedly. "Sorry, boy, you can't come with me. You need to stay with Mommy."

She took hold of the leash and watched him trudge up the steps toward the top of the big twisty slide, his hair bouncing up and down in the breeze.

The first time Danny had come to Ethan Allen Park was after the divorce. Drew had taken him for the day. When he came home, he regaled her with every exciting detail. He and Drew had spent hours exploring the park, from the playground to the trails, and even Ethan Allen Tower.

Between playing and walking around, Drew had made sure to talk to him about the divorce, explain it in simple terms. He told him that even though he and his mom still cared a lot about each other, they couldn't live in the same house anymore.

"It's no one's fault," Drew had said. "This is what's best for everyone."

The park had become a regular hangout for Danny and Drew. Each visit contained a new adventure for Danny to tell her about.

He slid down the slide for the third time.

"Hey, bud, are you ready to hike around for a bit?"

He nodded, too out of breath to speak.

They headed for the trail, made a slow loop through the park, munching on snacks from time to time, until they were back at the entrance parking lot.

"Mommy, I'm hungry."

"Hungry?" She laughed. "You mean that ziplock bag of Cheez-Its and Teddy Grahams weren't enough?"

"I'm a growing boy, you know."

"Where do you feel like going for lunch?"

"Handy's. Yay."

"That's not far from Aunt Melanie's. Should I invite her to meet us there?"

"Tell her to bring something sweet."

"How about a small box of muffins?" She opened the car door for him and waited until he buckled himself in. "We can eat them for breakfast tomorrow."

"What kind of muffins?"

She got in behind the wheel. "I'm thinking blueberry, banana, or apple-cinnamon."

"Yay. Apple." He threw his arms up and kicked the back of her seat.

"Ow. Watch where you're kicking, bud."

"Sorry, Mommy."

"I know you're excited. But you need to be careful." She leaned over to the passenger side, picked her backpack up off the floor, and unzipped it to get out her phone.

"Can Snowball get a treat?"

"Not this time."

Snowball whimpered.

"Sorry, boy. I tried," she heard him say as she texted Melanie. It took her less than a minute to respond: *'See you at Handy's with muffins in hand.'*

She backed out of the parking space, then put the car in drive, and headed toward the exit on North Avenue.

"I already know what I want for lunch." Danny's voice brimmed with enthusiasm.

"Oh yeah?"

"Grilled cheese with French Fries."

"That does sound good."

"You should get one, too, Mommy."

"I'll have to look at the menu." In her rearview mirror, she could see that his pearly whites were still on display.

Her plan had worked; her son was happy. He'd mentioned Drew only once when he was recalling the last time they'd walked the park. "We were looking for bugs," he'd said. "I found three, but Daddy wouldn't let me take them home, said you would be grateful for that."

Led by Her Heart

Lynn drove home first, to drop off Snowball.

"We'll be back soon," she said to the whimpering dog. "I promise."

Danny crouched down and gave Snowball a kiss on the head. "See you later, boy."

When they got back in the car, "I don't know about you, but I'm starving," she said.

"Me too."

As she was driving to *Handy's Lunch* to meet Melanie, Lynn wondered what the night would bring for Danny. Would he drift into dreamland, surrounded by cute puppies and friendly dinosaurs? Or would he once again be plagued with images of Drew's lifeless body?

Puppies and dinosaurs. Puppies and dinosaurs. Please.

Chapter 14

L ynn parked her car across the street from *Handy's Lunch*. She and Danny were frequent customers of the cozy, family-owned eatery, which was usually packed with locals. The staff never failed to make their patrons feel like family.

Melanie arrived seconds after Lynn, securing a parking space behind her car on the crowded street across from the restaurant.

"Hi, Aunt Melanie. Did you bring the muffins?"

She chuckled. "I sure did." She opened the passenger side door and took the box of breakfast treats off the seat. "Here you go, kiddo."

He opened the lid, and his eyes grew wide. "Those look yummy." He stared inside the box for a few seconds, then closed the lid, and turned around to face Lynn. "Here you go, Mommy."

Lynn put the box in her car, then reached into her backpack for her wallet. She took out twelve dollars for the muffins and handed it to Melanie.

"Thanks. This will go towards our lunch." She shoved the money into her jeans pocket.

"Let's go." Danny reached for his mom's hand. "I'm so hungry."

"He's a bottomless pit, I swear."

Melanie laughed.

When they walked into the brightly lit restaurant, there were just a few open stools in front of the wide horseshoe counter. As they were taking their seats, Lynn caught a whiff of someone's cheeseburger order. The juicy beef patty was glistening between the shelter of a toasted bun, and steam was rising from the top of golden cooked fries.

The owner was quick to greet them. Looking at Lynn and Danny, he said, "This is a nice surprise. I usually see you on weekends."

She smiled. "We decided to make an exception today."

"I'm glad you did." He placed three menus on the counter. "Jessica will be over shortly to take your order."

Lynn didn't recognize the name. She must have been a new hire.

"What to choose, what to choose," Melanie muttered, as she perused her menu. "Oh, the Texas double cheeseburger." She licked her lips in an exaggerated way. "Yes, please."

Danny laughed at her antics.

"Then again..." She looked down at her white V-neck blouse, then shrugged. "Yeah, it's worth the risk."

"Grilled cheese with French Fries for me," Danny said. "What do you want, Mommy?"

"Hmm. I don't know yet." She was trying to decide between a classic cheeseburger or a veggie burger when a woman boasting the 'Rachel' haircut modernized with blue and purple highlights came to the counter.

"Hi, everyone. My name is Jessica. I'll be your waitress for today. Can I start you off with something to drink?"

Danny raised his hand. "Can I have chocolate milk?"

"Sure thing, honey." She made a note on her tablet, then turned to Lynn. "And for you?"

"Just a water please."

"Okay." Jessica looked at Melanie. "Last but not least..."

"I'll have a soda, thank you."

"I'll be right back with those drinks."

"Hey, miss picky," Melanie said to Lynn. "Have you decided what you want for lunch?"

She laughed. "When have I ever been a picky eater? And yes. I'm going to stick with the classic cheeseburger."

"Seriously? Come on. Live a little. Get the Texas double cheeseburger, like me."

Lynn scrunched up her face. "That's a heart attack waiting to happen."

"You're no fun," Melanie quipped back.

Jessica returned with their drinks. "Are you ready to order?"

"We're ready," Melanie said.

Shortly after they placed their orders, Danny turned and looked at his mom. "I have to use the bathroom."

"Okay, honey. You know where it is."

He jumped off his stool, then started hippity-hopping away as if he were riding a horse.

Lynn leaned in toward Melanie conspiratorially. "Okay, I have to say this before he comes back."

Melanie's eyes grew wide with intrigue.

"I had a dream last night, about the P.I. I hired to find Drew." She could feel her cheeks flush.

"A sexy dream, I assume?"

"Oh yeah." Her body started to tingle.

"Shut the front door."

"Except, I woke up just before the good stuff started."

"The sex, Lynn? It's okay to say the word *sex*."

"It doesn't matter. I feel so guilty."

Melanie frowned. "About what?"

"Drew is missing, and here I am fantasizing about the man who's trying to find him. What does that say about me?"

"Uh, you're human. You have needs. It was just a dream, not like you went to his office, stripped naked, and had sex with him on his desk."

"I'm being serious, Melanie."

"So am I. You're doing everything you can to bring Drew home. Cut yourself some slack."

"But I wanted him to ravage me."

"You go, girl."

"Even after I woke up."

"Alright. If you have any more dreams like that, feel free to share them. It's been a while for me."

Lynn burst out laughing. "You're so bad." She saw Danny riding his imaginary pony back to the table, nearly colliding with another customer.

"Danny, honey, be careful."

Jessica delivered their orders as Danny was taking his seat at the counter. She placed the plates in front of them, one by one, starting with Danny's grilled cheese. He immediately dove in, fries first.

After taking a bite of her beloved Texas double cheeseburger, Melanie closed her eyes. "Mmm, so good."

Lynn chuckled. If Danny wasn't with them, she'd make a joke that would be deemed inappropriate. Instead, she kept quiet and enjoyed her lunch, though not as much as Melanie, it appeared.

As they stood from their stools, ready to leave the restaurant, a familiar looking woman walked in and took a seat at the counter, not far from Lynn. It was Drew's ex-girlfriend, Theresa Lambert. Lynn noticed how stunning she looked with her porcelain skin and dark waist-length hair and curtain bangs that gave applause to her perfectly shaped eyebrows. But it was Theresa's crystal blue eyes that brought everything together.

She contemplated saying 'hello.' It was clear, from the sheet of paper and pen Theresa took out of her bag, that she was busy. Lynn decided to leave her be, but Theresa spotted her.

"Lynn. Lynn Callahan."

"Theresa? I thought I recognized you."

She looked from Lynn to her son and waved. "Hi, Danny."

He ducked behind Lynn's leg as her gaze landed on the silver dragonfly chain around Theresa's neck, a complement to her denim shirt.

"How have you been?"

"Good—" she started but her phone rang. She reached into her bag, pulled out her phone, and looked at the display. After exhaling a huff, she declined the call, then turned the phone face-down on the counter next to the sheet of paper. "Sorry about that. I've been good, considering."

"Are you meeting someone here for lunch?"

"I'm looking for work." She held up the paper: *Job Application*. "Addiction ruined more than my relationship with Drew." She looked from Lynn to Danny and back again. "Have you heard anything?"

"Melanie," Lynn called and tipped her head to Danny. "Please take him to the car. I'll be out shortly."

"Sure. Come on, kiddo." Melanie took his hand and led him out of the restaurant.

Lynn sat next to Theresa. "I hired a P.I."

She showed her a wan smile. "I figured it was you who had given him my name."

Lynn raised her hand. "Guilty."

"It doesn't feel real. I just talked to him a couple weeks ago. You probably know that."

"I know you two spoke, but I don't know what about."

Theresa shook her head. "I called to thank him, tell him I entered an NA program. It took me hitting rock bottom first. Then I remembered Drew's words, how he urged me to get help from Narcotics Anonymous, that it would save my life."

"Drew really did care about you."

"I owe him a debt I can never repay."

As they were talking, Lynn came to a chilling realization. When Jake called her yesterday, he'd said Dale had stopped going to meetings last year, just before Theresa and Drew started dating, and before Theresa relapsed. Was it possible that Dale and Theresa knew each other from NA? She didn't want to believe that Theresa could be involved in Drew's disappearance, but she needed to examine the case from every possible angle.

Please let this one be a dead end.

Theresa's phone rang again. She flipped it over, declined the call then switched the mode to silent.

"Why didn't you answer that call?"

"It's just an ex. We broke up after I entered the program. He's not happy about it."

"Why not?"

"Birds of a feather...you know...flock together. I dropped out of the flock and he wants me back in."

Lynn squinted with concern for Theresa's safety. "Maybe you should call the police...get a protective order..."

"He's harmless. I just can't be associated with

anyone who can bring me back down."

"I wish you luck with that...just be careful."

"I almost called Drew again, on Thursday night. I wanted to talk to someone who knew what I was going through, hoped he would let me come over, but I stopped myself. With him having a new girlfriend, and all, I figured that would be inappropriate." She rubbed her hands together. "I wish I could go back in time, make that call, go to see him...maybe I could have helped him." Tears welled in her blue eyes.

Lynn reached for Theresa's trembling hands to still them. This woman was either an emotional wreck or an Oscar-winning actor. "I'll call you if I hear anything else."

"Thank you, Lynn. I feel better that you're on the case."

She stood to leave, and as she walked to her car, she replayed the conversation with Theresa in her head. There was genuine concern there. Theresa didn't act like someone who was harboring guilt, more like someone who'd lost a loved one.

But the phone calls she'd declined. Those were suspicious. Theresa said it was an ex drug buddy. If that was true, was he as harmless as Theresa believed?

Chapter 15

Lynn started her car, prepared to go home, when Danny said, "Mommy, do you think Daddy came back home and forgot to call us?"

More difficult questions.

"I don't think he would forget to call. That doesn't sound like your daddy."

"Maybe this time he did. You forget things."

"Hey, that's not fair," she teased.

"Well, you do," he said bluntly.

"I think, when Daddy comes home, you will be the first person he calls."

"Can we go to his apartment? Just to see if he's there. Please?"

Lynn knew Drew wouldn't be there. Going to his apartment would only cause Danny more pain. "We need to get back home to Snowball. He probably needs a walk."

"Oh." He hung his head low.

"I'll tell you what. We'll take the long way home, so we can pass by Daddy's apartment building to see if his car is there."

Danny lifted his head and smiled. "Okay."

She drove straight to Drew's apartment building. At the traffic light to the parking lot, she put on her right turn signal. As she made the turn, a tan Honda sedan was pulling out. It had a University of Vermont bumper sticker on it. She thought it had to be the same car Drew's neighbor saw, the same sedan caught on the traffic cam. It had to be Ray Jackson's.

She took a mental note of the Honda's license plate. *Gotcha, Ray.*

***

When they got back from walking Snowball, Danny headed for the living room and turned on the TV while the pup made a beeline for his water bowl.

"I'll be right back, bud. I need to make a call in my bedroom. Watch Snowball, okay?"

Danny nodded, his eyes glued to the TV, his mouth open slightly.

She closed her bedroom door then called Jake's cell phone number.

"Hey, I was just about to call you."

"What's new?"

"Charlie's alibis check out, but that doesn't mean he's not involved. He could have had Ray do his dirty work. I'm going to take another crack at Ray's roommate, David, get him to realize that covering for Ray is useless, not to mention criminal."

"You may not need to do that." She told Jake about the tan Honda with the university bumper sticker and gave him the plate number.

"Nice work. This could be what we need to crack Ray and get him to give up his partner...the guy driving Drew's car."

"Let's hope. Oh, by the way, I saw Drew's ex, Theresa, today. I hope I'm wrong about this, but there's a possibility that she and Dale may have attended the same Narcotics Anonymous meetings. The timeline fits."

"I'll look into it, see what I can find out."

She sighed. "It's a long shot, I know."

"Hey, we're closer now than we've ever been to finding Drew. Why do you sound so glum?"

She exhaled slowly. "I'm confused. Whoever took Drew went through a lot of trouble to make it look like he relapsed and left town, but why would Ray return to Drew's apartment?"

"Sounds stupid to me. Maybe we're giving them too much credit."

"Yeah...unless." Lynn had an ah-ha moment. "Oh, man. That's it. I should have known."

"You want to clue me in?"

"The empty pill bottles in Drew's apartment. Whoever was driving the Honda must have come back to get them."

"Why? They've served their purpose to mislead the investigation."

"Those bottles may have fingerprints and DNA on them that aren't Drew's."

"Surely the culprits wiped them clean."

"Maybe they didn't. I need to go back there to see if the bottles are gone. I'll call you later."

"Lynn. Wait. Don't go without—"

She ended the call then dialed her neighbor. "Ellen. It's Lynn next door. I know this is last minute, but could you come by and watch Danny for a little while?"

"Why? What's up? Did they find Drew?"

"Not yet, but I have to follow a clue. Less than an hour, I'm sure."

"I'll be right there."

"Thanks. You're the best."

***

When Lynn arrived at Drew's apartment, she unlocked the door and walked straight into the living room. Sure enough, the empty pill bottles that Officer Grayson had placed on the kitchen counter were gone.

She took her phone out and called Jake. "I was

right. The pill bottles aren't here."

"You have good instincts."

"It's got to be Ray," she said with conviction. "But his partner, the one calling the shots, is a mystery. I still think it's Charlie. He's got the motive."

"As does anyone connected to Dale Hogan. I called his former roommate, Trevor Dawson. He has solid alibis for both Thursday night and Friday morning. I left a voice mail with Mike Rowland, and I'm meeting with Alex Murphy tomorrow afternoon. He claims to be Dale's best friend."

"What about a girlfriend? Anything there?"

"Girlfriend? Good idea. I hadn't thought outside the family and friends box. Alex Murphy should know if Dale had a girlfriend. I'll be sure to ask him. Call you tomorrow."

When Lynn got off the phone with Jake, she took a seat on Drew's living room couch and exhaled deeply. Jake was right. The suspects weren't so smart. Not a mastermind among them. Ray took a big risk coming back to the apartment. He may have been smart enough to remove the license plates the first time but forgot to remove them on the return trip. Sloppy and amateurish.

We are closing in on you, Ray.

Chapter 16

The next morning, while Lynn was on her way to work—after getting coffee for her and Angela at Starbuck's—her phone rang. "Jake. What do you got?"

"The license plate number is a match to Ray's Honda."

"I knew it." She wanted to pull over and do a happy dance on the highway.

"I'm on my way to the university to confront him."

"Can you make him give up his partner...you know...by jamming pins under his fingernails?"

"I prefer water-boarding, myself."

"Seriously?"

"We may not have proof that Drew was kidnapped, but we do have proof that it was Ray's car behind Drew's in the traffic cam footage. Circumstantial evidence can put him behind the wheel. Ray's grudge against Drew for a bad grade is weak motivation, but I'm confident I can convince him to fold."

"Then you won't need to talk to Alex Murphy."

"He's expecting me, and I'll leave no stone left unturned. He may know something, being Dale's best friend, and all."

"Good luck." She ended the call and took a deep breath. "This is good, really good." A two-ton weight had been lifted from her shoulders. The case was coming to a close. What better way to celebrate than auditioning party bands that catered to Billy Joel fans.

***

When Lynn walked into the office, she greeted Angela with one of the coffees she had brought.

Angela gasped lightly. "Bless your heart." She took a sip of her coffee, then exhaled with satisfaction.

She noticed Angela's bleary hazel eyes. "Rough night?"

Angela drew a few strands of her long red hair off her face. "The kids woke up at the crack of dawn, screaming and fighting. What else is new?"

Lynn chuckled. "Here's hoping that coffee kicks in soon."

"I'll drink to that." She raised the coffee cup to her lips and took another big sip.

Angela, like Lynn, was a single mom, but had two kids, both under the age of ten. Lynn had met them on various occasions, and each time, she thanked her lucky stars for Danny. He may have been rambunctious at times, but he listened to her, for the most part, and he was always good in public places.

On the way to her office, Lynn stopped by Cassidy's cubicle. "How did everything work out with the Powell party dilemma?"

Her smile was wide and her eyes bright and worry free. "I called Mrs. Powell and explained the band problem. She took the news better than I expected. After that, I made a few calls and was able to book a D.J."

"That's great. Another happy client."

"I've had to put out a few other fires since then, but the issues have been resolved and the party is back on track."

"Keep that confidence. It looks good on you."

Lynn strolled into her office and sat behind her desk. Emails were piling up. She'd no sooner set her coffee aside when the intercom buzzed. "Someone by the name of Charlie Benson is here to see you. Should I send him in?"

Her jaw clenched. What the hell was that backstabbing weasel doing here? No way did she want to see him. "Angela, tell him I'm busy and that I have no time to see him."

"He's demanding to see you now."

"Call security and have him removed."

"Sir. Sir. You can't go in there."

The door flew open, and a man stormed in. She was shocked at his appearance. The well-groomed professor she remembered, who always wore button-downs, power ties, and crisply ironed slacks, was nothing but a memory. Standing in his place was a derelict who'd lost the desire for basic hygiene. He had on a stained, wrinkled t-shirt, ripped jeans, and beat up sneakers. His unkempt hair looked oily, and a ragged beard and dark circles under his once electric blue eyes added to his look of misery.

"Lynn, please. I've got to talk to you." He held his hands up, palms out, as if saying he'd keep his distance.

She stood, shoulders back, scowling. "What do you want from me, Charlie? Haven't you taken enough?"

"I assume you know everything that went down at the university."

"You betrayed your best friend, lied to me about working there, and feigned concern for Drew's safety." She set her hands flat on her desk and leaned forward. "Get out of my sight."

"I get it. I lied. You're mad. Okay? But you must believe me. I don't know where Drew went, and I certainly would never hurt him."

"Hurt him? No. Of course not. You accused him of doing drugs again, tried to get him fired. That wouldn't hurt him, it'd ruin his life."

"I was angry, Lynn." He raised his voice. "Drew ratted me out, got me fired. Me..." he slapped the center of his chest, "his best friend. Who betrayed who first?"

"You lost your temper and upended a desk. A student could have been injured."

"Nobody got hurt. I didn't hit anyone. I lost my temper, but Drew made a big deal of it."

"He was only thinking of those students. And what about you, Charlie? I've never known you to be an angry man. What happened?"

He exhaled. "Roxanne and I have been having problems for a while now, all over my job, grading my students' papers well past midnight. She threatened to move out, take the kids with her. I got frustrated...threw the chair. She was willing to work things out, until I got fired, thanks to Drew. Now she wants a divorce, and my kids don't know what to think."

"All good reasons to blame Drew. Do you really expect me to believe that you didn't want revenge?"

"Angry with him or not, Drew's still my best

friend. I had nothing to do with his disappearance, Lynn. You have no reason to sic a P.I. on me."

"That's a sad story, Charlie, but the only one who knows the truth is Drew. So, you better pray we find him...alive and well. Now get out of my office before I have security throw you out."

"Lynn, please—"

"I said go," she yelled and pointed to the door.

Charlie waved his hands in defeat. "Fine. I'm going, but if you get the chance, tell Drew I'm sorry."

After he left, she fell into her chair, her heart racing and her body shaking. What if Charlie was telling the truth? Jake had said his alibis checked out. However, he had a strong motive. His marriage was over, in his mind, because of Drew. Her eyes widened. "Roxanne." She had good reason to be angry with Drew. If Ray named her as his partner, Lynn wouldn't be surprised.

She placed her head down on her desk and closed her eyes. "Oh, Billy Joel, save me with your music."

Alert to the sound of approaching footsteps outside her office, she raised her head slowly, then came a gentle knock on the door. "Lynn?"

"Come in."

Angela opened the door and stepped in,

frowning. "What was all that yelling about?"

"I really don't like that guy."

"Who was he?"

"No one important."

"Violet Miller is here. Do you need a few minutes?"

"That won't be necessary. I'm fine." She followed Angela to the atrium where Violet was waiting.

"Morning, Lynn," Violet said with a big smile. "I couldn't remember if our meeting was for ten or ten-thirty, so I went with the former."

"You're right on time. The first band should be arriving shortly. Follow me." They took the elevator down to the basement, Lynn's staging area. There was a large table in the center of the room with two chairs. "Have a seat. I'll be right back."

She opened the loading door for *Our Life*: five men, all skinny, and in their mid-to-late thirties. "You guys can set up over there." She pointed to a low platform stationed twenty feet from the table where she would be sitting with Violet.

Lynn sat next to her while the band set up their equipment.

"*This* is a Billy Joel fan band?" Violet whispered. She scrunched her eyebrows together. "Do they even know who Billy Joel is?"

"Trust me." She had done her homework. *Our Life* was more than qualified for an audition. "What song will you be playing for us?" she asked the lead singer. He was on the shorter side, with a full head of dark brown hair. He had Joel's younger look down solid.

"*Tell Her About It*," the singer said in a deep voice.

"Okay. Whenever you're ready."

He took a few steps back, then gave a nod to his band members.

She glanced at Violet, who was still frowning, with her arms crossed, until the trumpets sounded. Her eyes softened a bit, eyebrows less clenched.

The singer ran to the microphone and belted out the first high note with perfect pitch. He never missed a beat as he moved his hips from side to side and his arms back and forth.

Lynn caught Violet out of the corner of her eye, smiling and swaying to the music. "Wow. They're good."

When the song finished, Lynn stood. "Thank you, guys. I'll be in touch."

Ten minutes later, the next band arrived, *Easy Music*. They were good, nice stage presence, but they weren't quite as good as *Our Life*, nor was the third and final band, *Borderline*.

"So..." Lynn said to Violet when the last band left. "What do you think?"

"Hands down. *Our Life.*"

"Great. I'll give them a call and let them know they got the gig."

"My mother's going to love them. You're a genius."

She grinned. "It's not that big a deal."

Lynn and Violet took the elevator back up to the main level, then Violet left, and Lynn headed up to her top floor office.

At quitting time, she expected her shoulders to tense up and her chest to tighten, as they had every day for the past week after work. Instead, she remained calm and at peace because Jake was going to call her soon with good news about Drew.

Her heart was telling her that he was alive and would be home tonight.

Come on, heart. Don't let me down.

Chapter 17

As Lynn was preparing dinner for her and Danny, baked ziti with garlic bread and a salad, her phone rang. She placed the pan of ziti in the oven and set the timer for thirty minutes, then she strode to the kitchen table and picked up her phone. *Jake's Cell* showed on the display.

"Hey, how did everything go with Ray? Did he tell you what happened to Drew?"

"Are you home right now?" There was an urgency in his tone.

The calm Lynn was feeling earlier was fading fast. "Yeah. I'm cooking dinner."

"Can you be ready in five minutes?"

"Ready? Ready for what?" Lynn's heart started to pound. "Did you find Drew?"

"Sort of."

"Sort of? What the hell does that mean?"

"I'll explain everything when I pick you up."

"I'll be ready." She hung up then called Melanie. "Jake wants to see me about Drew. Can you watch Danny right now?"

"I'm on my way."

Lynn walked to her front door and stared out the window while she waited for Jake and Melanie. She wasn't sure how to feel. Happy? Relieved? Jake was so evasive.

***

When Jake pulled up, he was on the phone with someone as Lynn raced to his car. He motioned for her to get in.

"Okay, thanks, man. We're on our way."

"On our way where? Jake, what's going on?"

"I spoke with Ray..." Jake pulled away from the curb and headed up Hillcrest toward Hedge Road. "He was tightlipped and defiant."

"He didn't confess?"

"Not at first, not until I found the empty pill bottles on him. Then he sang like a canary. Turns out, he was hired to get Drew to go with him Thursday night. Gave up his partner, too, David Lane."

"His roommate? *He* was behind all of this?"

"No. They were both hired."

"Well..? Who hired them?"

"You're not going to believe it."

"At this point I'd believe the Pope did it."

"It's Beth Meyers."

"Beth Meyers? Drew's new girlfriend? Why?"

"Because she's really Dale's girlfriend. When I spoke with his friend, Alex Murphy, he told me Beth and Dale had been dating for a year before the car crash."

Lynn slumped down in her seat to process this new information. "It doesn't make any sense. You said it yourself. Her alibi checked out. I heard the desperation in her voice. It was all an act?"

"I spoke with her friends again. She was at the movie with them, alright, but left thirty minutes early. David Lane drove Drew's car, handed him off to Beth, then drove to the train station to ditch the car. Ray picked him up down the road."

She scowled. "What did they do with Drew? Where is he?"

"It turns out Beth's father owns a shuttered metalworks building on Flynn Avenue, less than two miles south of Drew's apartment. Perfect place to take a hostage."

"Is that where we're going?"

"Yeah." Jake turned on Shelburn heading south. "I called a contact at the station. He got a search warrant based on Ray's confession."

Arriving at the sprawling metalworks company, they encountered bright flashing lights: three cop cars, and an ambulance in the parking lot. Paramedics were wheeling a stretcher out of the building.

Jake had barely stopped the car before Lynn bailed out. "Drew," she screamed as she ran toward the ambulance. Tears flooded her face when she saw him on the stretcher, moaning and badly beaten, his face bloodied and his right eye swollen shut. She grabbed his hand and sobbed out, "My god. Drew."

He turned his head weakly. Confusion emanated from his one open eye. "Lynn? Is that you?"

Her heart sank. "Yes, Drew. It's me. Danny's going to be so happy. We found you. We found you."

An EMT motioned for her to back off. "Ma'am, we need to get him to the hospital right away."

She let go of his hand so they could load him into the ambulance, then pressed toward the door. "I want to go with him."

The EMT held her back. "There's nothing you can do for him now."

"How bad is it?"

"Other than the obvious blunt-force trauma, he's been drugged, an overdose of heroin. It took two doses of Narcan to bring him around. He needs time to recover. Check with the doctors tomorrow."

"Okay. Of course." She stepped back. The doors closed, and the ambulance sped off. As she watched the flashing lights recede down Flynn, she felt a hand on her shoulder, turned around slowly, and locked eyes with Jake. All she wanted to do was fall into his arms and allow his soft touch to ease her despair for Drew.

"Come on." He turned her toward the car. "Let's get out of here."

She saw an officer walking a handcuffed Beth toward a patrol car. Rage took over. She screamed, tore away from Jake, and charged toward Beth with every intention of beating her to death.

"Lynn, wait. No," Jake yelled.

The officer pulled his service revolver. "Stop." He was duty-bound to protect his prisoner.

She was seconds from getting shot when Jake grabbed her waist and yanked her away from Beth.

"I'll kill you. I'll kill you, bitch." She pushed herself forward, fists swinging at the air as she tried to break through Jake's grip.

"It's over, Lynn. It's over."

"Let me go," she screamed. Tears streamed down her face. "She nearly killed Drew. And I'm supposed to do nothing?" She tried to squirm out of Jake's hold. "I'll scratch her eyes out."

He spun her around. "She's not worth it, Lynn. Think of Danny."

The officer pushed Beth into the car and

slammed the door.

"Our job is done, Lynn. They'll handle it from here."

She collapsed to the ground. "It's not fair," she cried. "It's just not fair."

He helped her up, placed his arm around her waist, and with her head tilted against the right side of his chest, they walked to his car.

A CSI van pulled in, and techs in white suits piled out, each carrying cases of equipment.

Jake started the car. "It's going to be a long night for those guys."

Back on Flynn Road, she stared out the window and noticed they weren't heading in the direction of her house. He was probably taking her to the station to give them an official statement, but he was driving south on Shelburne instead of north. She thought back to that moment she'd wanted to kill Beth. If Jake hadn't stopped her, there was no telling how bad things would have turned. And then what? If she'd given her what she had coming, assault and battery, she'd have lost Danny and destroyed her career. Worse, she could have been shot and body-bagged for the morgue.

Thank God for Jake.

Chapter 18

L ynn sat across from Jake at a table, not in a police interrogation room, but inside Shy Guy Gelato on Saint Paul Street. She dug a plastic spoon into her cup of Black Forest Cake, topped with Amarena cherries and chocolate chunks, and slowly put the creamy delight into her mouth. Closing her eyes, she sighed. *Heaven on a spoon.* "Thank you for this," she said after her second spoonful melted on her tongue.

"Ice cream is the ultimate comfort food..." He ploughed his spoon into his Choco-Palooza. "For me, at least."

"A man after my own heart."

"So, you're feeling better, then?"

"I've never been so mad in my life."

"We can talk about it if you want."

"I just can't...can't stop thinking about Drew and everything he went through this week." She spooned more ice cream. "Then there's Danny. What am I supposed to say when he asks to visit Drew in the hospital? You saw what he looked like. I can't let

Danny see his dad all bruised and bloodied."

"Tell him the truth without telling him everything. His dad is okay but isn't feeling well, and that you'll go see him when he's ready for visitors."

"Yeah. Yeah, that's good. Should hold him off, for a little while anyway."

Jake spooned more ice cream. "Glad I could help."

"For someone who doesn't have kids, you give pretty good advice about them."

He furrowed his brows. "What makes you think I don't have kids?"

"Oh, you do?" She lowered her eyes, a bit embarrassed that she'd jumped to that conclusion. "I-I didn't see any pictures of kids in your office, so I just assumed... I'm going to stop talking now."

Jake licked his spoon. "You assumed right. I don't have any kids right now, but some day, maybe, with the right woman."

Her heart fluttered. She hadn't known Jake for more than a week, but the effect his presence had on her felt like she'd known him for years. It wasn't just his soft deep voice, but the way he licked that spoon gave her the chills. My god, that tongue...

Ice cream gone and with her nerves settled, she followed Jake back to his car. Once inside, she sent

Melanie a text: *'We're on our way back.'*

'Did you find Drew?'

'I'll tell you about it when I get there.'

'Take your time. Danny's in bed.'

She turned to Jake and smiled. "Danny's asleep."

He looked at her and laughed.

"What? Why are you laughing?"

"Some kids never grow up." He reached over and pulled the visor down. "Look." The lighted mirror revealed tiny morsels of chocolate on the corners of her mouth.

"Oh, ha-ha. I was saving them for a midnight snack." She reached to wipe them off, but he blocked her hand.

"Allow me." He placed his palm gently on her cheek and dabbed the crumbs away with his thumb, sending shivers up her spine and loosing butterflies in her tummy. She remembered that sexy dream. The wave of warmth that spread through her, the way her body tightened when his bare chest touched hers.

The moment lingered with his hand on her cheek. The warmth of his touch, the aroma of his cologne, the beating of her heart all combined to set fires down below. She wanted him to take her, right then and there. She wanted the windows to steam up from their passion... But what if he didn't feel the same?

"I, uh..." He cleared his throat. "I better get you home." He pulled away quickly and started the car.

"Yeah," she said in a breathless whisper, but she didn't want to go home. She wanted to explore that moment, continue the connection, see where Jake would take it, but the mood was broken in the flow of traffic on Williston Road.

***

When Lynn and Jake walked in, Melanie sprang from the couch and rushed to the front door. "Hey." She wrapped Lynn in a tight hug. "Did you find Drew?"

Lynn pulled away. "We did. We found him. He's at the hospital now. I hope he won't be transferred to rehab."

Melanie placed a hand to her mouth. "Jeez. So, he did relapse?"

"Oh, no. Sorry. He...he was overdosed with heroin." She slipped her purse strap off her shoulder and handed it to Jake. "Could you put this on the kitchen table for me?"

"Sure."

As he walked to the kitchen, Melanie looped her arm around Lynn's shoulders and led her into the living room. They sat next to each other on the couch. "Tell me all about it."

Jake came in and sat in the chair across from them.

Melanie had not acknowledged his presence, so intent on Lynn as she was. "Who gave him heroin?"

"His new girlfriend, Beth Meyers. It turns out she's really Dale Hogan's girlfriend."

Melanie frowned. "Dale Hogan. I remember that name. You and Drew went to college with him, right?"

She nodded. "Dale reached out to Drew a few months ago. He wanted to get together, but Drew turned him down. Two nights after that, Dale took a fistful of pills, went for a ride, and crashed his car into a tree. He's been in a coma ever since."

"Let me guess. Beth blames Drew for Dale being comatose?"

She exhaled a shaky breath. "I can't get the image of him on the ambulance gurney out of my head." She started to choke up. "He was so badly beaten, Melanie. His face was covered in blood and his right eye was swollen shut."

Melanie gasped. "That poor man." Her chin quivered as if she was on the verge of tears.

"I went after Beth. I was this close to her." She demonstrated with her thumb and index finger. "If Jake hadn't stopped me, you'd probably be bailing me out of jail."

"It was nothing," Jake said.

Melanie turned to him. "Thank you. And not just for saving me money for her bond." She set a hand on Lynn's arm. "I wish I could stay but I need to get up early tomorrow. Are you going to be alright?"

"I'll be fine. Thanks for watching Danny."

"Any time." She stood.

Lynn walked her to the door, and Melanie pulled her into a warm embrace. "Call me when you know more about Drew's condition."

"I will."

She watched Melanie's car pull out of the driveway and fade away down Hillcrest. Back in the living room, she plopped herself onto the couch, buried her face in her hands, and let out a deep sigh. All it took was one conversation with Melanie to bring her back to the building where Drew had been found: beaten and barely conscious.

She lowered her hands and balled them into fists as she thought about the bitch who put Drew on that stretcher. She was consumed with anger, sadness, and worry.

Jake rose from the chair and sat beside her. "Hey, Lynn, come back." He placed one hand on her back and the other over her white-knuckled fist.

His gentle touch coaxed her fingers to uncurl, and she grabbed onto his hand like it was the ledge of a tall building. "I'm sorry, Jake. I'm not an angry person by nature. I just... When I think about what Beth did to Drew, all I see is darkness."

"Anger will do that." His hands continued circulating their power of comfort and calm. "But, hey, Drew is going to be okay."

"I want to believe that, but how much can one person take without breaking? What if he's addicted again?"

"I know it's hard, but Drew will overcome this, just like he has in the past."

"How can you be so sure?"

"Oh, I didn't tell you?" He leaned in close, his breath at her ear. "I'm psychic," he whispered.

"Psychic, huh?"

"Yup." He grinned. "I only moonlight as a private investigator."

"Is that so?"

"Okay, maybe not. But I do know that Drew will come out of this on the other side."

"Why are you so confident?"

"Because of you."

Her cheeks warmed and her heart started to beat faster. She was done with the *what ifs* and the *maybes*.

Time for action.

She slipped her hand out from under Jake's hand and reached around his neck, then pulled his face to hers. Their lips were microseconds away from joining when Jake leaned back. "We can't do this, Lynn."

Oh, no. He doesn't feel the same.

She shook her head. "I'm so sorry. I shouldn't have done that." If she could've made herself tiny, she would've crawled under the throw pillow. "I get it. Business. Strictly business."

"Not exactly—"

She rose from the couch, "How much do I owe you?" and headed into the kitchen to get her purse.

He was quick to follow her. "Lynn, wait. Let's talk."

She got out her checkbook. "How much?" Pen ready, she stared down at the check through teary eyes. She felt like such a fool, throwing herself on him. All she wanted now was to settle up and be rid of her embarrassment.

Jake placed his hand over the check on the table, but she kept her head down. "Will you look at me? Please?"

She looked up. "I get it. I know. There's nothing to talk about. Let's just forget this ever happened. I hired you to do the job. You did it successfully. End of story."

He took her lightly by the arm. "Lynn, look at me."

She didn't want to hear it. *"You're a great girl, but I just don't see you in that way..."* or another polite version of the same rejection.

"I like you, Lynn. And I really did want to kiss you."

"You pulled away. I got the message."

"You've been through a lot this week. Then, tonight, finally finding Drew, and in bad condition, it's understandable you'd reach out, but you're not in the right headspace."

"What do you know about my headspace?" She glared at him. "You can't decide that for me."

"Look, if you wake up tomorrow with a clear head, and you still want to see me, call me." He reached to the table and closed the checkbook. "You don't owe me any more money. The retainer covered everything." He turned and strode to the door.

"Good night, Jake," she said in a soft voice. "I really am sorry I screwed up everything."

"Sleep well, Lynn." And he was gone out the door, now a mere shadow in the night as he got into his car.

She watched him drive away, shook off the

disappointment in her heart, and then made two phone calls: first to Andrea, then to Theresa. Once she was off the phone, she checked the locks on the doors, turned off the porch light and living room lights, then headed to her bedroom. On the way, she stopped to peak into Danny's room, saw him sleeping without a care in the world with Snowball curled up at his feet. "Everything is going to be okay," she whispered and blew them a kiss.

After changing into her pajamas, she snuggled under her sheets and laid her head on her pillow. Before she turned off the lamp on her nightstand, she thought about what Jake had said. He was right. Her emotions were all over the place.

She was sad for Drew, worried about his recovery, unsure of how Danny would react to the situation, and angry that it happened in the first place. She was never one to believe in fate or destiny, but she started to wonder. Could she and Jake be meant for each other? Was Drew put through hell so she could meet Jake? Or was it all for not over a misguided kiss?

Chapter 19

Lynn spent the weekend busying herself and Danny. On Saturday, they watched a movie and threw a dance party in the living room, and on Sunday, they went for a hike with Snowball at Shelburne Farms. When Danny asked about seeing his dad, she followed Jake's advice.

"He isn't feeling well right now."

"So, he needs to be alone?"

"He needs to rest before he can have visitors."

"Can I make him a get-well card?"

"That's a great idea, bud."

"I'll draw a T-rex doctor taking care of his Stegosaurus patient."

"Daddy loves your artwork. It'll be a masterpiece, I'm sure."

On Sunday night, after Danny had gone to bed, Lynn called the hospital.

"UVM Medical Center."

"I'm calling about a patient, Drew Callahan. He was admitted Friday night. Could you tell me what room he's in?"

"Mr. Callahan is in the ICU. Would you like me to transfer you?"

"Could you, please? Thank you."

"ICU."

"Is Drew Callahan allowed to have visitors?"

"Are you family?"

"He's my ex...my son's father. I'm Lynn Callahan. Can you give me an update on his condition?"

"He's in pretty bad shape. Heavily sedated. He suffered severe lacerations to his face and internal injuries to his abdomen."

She frowned. "His abdomen?"

"Blunt force trauma."

She swallowed hard. "Oh, jeez. I really need to see him."

"I understand, but he might not know you're there. Next week would be better. By then he should be awake and recovered enough to be discharged. We're recommending that he enters the rehab program at River Rock Treatment."

River Rock. Lynn knew the outpatient center well. Drew had been treated there a few times over the years. "Alright. I'll visit him next week. If he wakes up, tell him, okay?"

"I'm sure he'll be happy to know you're stopping by."

"Thanks." She hung up.

***

She'd hoped to visit Drew on Monday evening, after she got off work, but two of her employees called out with a stomach bug, leaving Lynn busier than usual. She phoned the ICU. He still wasn't awake. By Wednesday, her schedule returned to its usual pace, and the ICU reported Drew was up and receiving visitors in Recovery on the fifth floor.

She called Andrea. "Can you watch Danny after school while I go to the hospital to visit Drew?"

"Sure. I'll meet him at the bus stop in front of your house and take him to my house. The three of us can have dinner together afterward."

"I'll see you then." She ended the call and placed the phone on her desk, then she focused her attention on the checklist she'd made for Violet's party. The venue was confirmed, and the menu was set; the band had been hired; the decorations had been purchased. Still to do: order tablecloths, contact Lindsey Hart about the custom poster, and call the florist.

She started from the bottom of the list, using her office phone to call Chappell's Florist on Williston Road. She'd used their services several times in the past and was a firm believer in the saying, 'if it ain't broke, don't fix it.'

After completing the rest of her checklist and answering a series of questions from several of her employees, Lynn shut down her computer. Instead of her usual sense of satisfaction after a productive day, she felt...bored. It all seemed so trivial.

Goodbye work. Hello Drew.

She parked on the second level of the hospital's main campus parking garage, grabbed her purse off the passenger seat, and headed toward the East pavilion. Once inside, she took the elevator to the fifth floor and followed the signs to Recovery.

"I'm here to see Drew Callahan," she told the duty nurse.

"Second room on the right."

"Thanks." As Lynn approached Drew's room, Theresa walked out. "This is a nice surprise."

"I came to cheer him up. Instead, he's the one who made me smile. He's incredible."

"You'll get no argument from me there."

Theresa placed her hand on Lynn's arm. "Tell Danny I said hi."

"Of course. Any luck with finding a job?"

She forced a smile. "Where there's sobriety, there's hope." With that, she walked out of Recovery, head high as if she meant those words wholeheartedly.

Dreading what she might see, Drew wrapped in

bandages like a mummy with tubes and wires going every-which-way, Lynn entered his room, determined not to show him how nervous and scared she felt. He looked worse than she'd imagined. The cuts and bruises on his face were not bandaged, looked black and blue and greasy from antiseptic gel, and his right eye was still swollen shut. He was shirtless, revealing a heavily bandaged abdomen, no doubt from the surgery required to repair his internal injuries. Wires ran from his chest to a heart monitor that beeped steadily. "My God, Drew. You're a mess."

"And you're a sight for sore eyes." His voice was hoarse as he pointed to his bad eye. "Don't just stand there gawking." He motioned for her to come closer.

Her smile was tested when she got to Drew's bedside. She noticed cuts on his hands that she hadn't seen Friday night.

"You should've seen the other guy," he quipped.

She forced back a flood of tears. "I would have come earlier today but..." She started to choke up. "So, umm, I saw Theresa in the hall."

"Yeah. She was checking up on me."

"How *are* you doing?"

"I thought I was going to die. Now I look like a zombie."

"You never looked better." She laughed.

Drew started to laugh but winced.

"Sorry."

"How's Danny doing?"

"He's worried, a little confused, but he mostly just misses his dad."

"I miss him too. I'm sorry. I'm so sorry." His hands started to shake.

"Drew, you have nothing to be sorry about." She steadied his trembling hands with hers. "You did nothing wrong. The blame is all on Beth. Your so-called girlfriend is the reason you're here."

"Boy, I sure know how to pick 'em, huh."

"After me, everything is downhill."

He coughed. "I can't help but wonder if Beth always had homicidal issues or if she just snapped...after Dale's suicide attempt." The heart monitor beeped faster. "I should have—"

"No." Lynn frowned. "Don't blame yourself for what happened to him."

"Don't get me wrong, I'm angry as hell...and I feel betrayed, but if I had agreed to meet with him, maybe he wouldn't be in a coma right now, and Beth wouldn't have gone off the deep end."

Lynn shook her head adamantly. "You didn't reject Dale out of cruelty. You were protecting your sobriety."

"I know...I just...I just wish things turned out differently for him. He almost made it, looking for atonement, and I shot him down."

"You're alive. That's what matters."

The heart monitor slowed. "I hear I have you to thank for that."

"I can't take all the credit."

"The private investigator. Connolly, right?" His hands stopped shaking.

"He did what the cops wouldn't do. How'd you know about him?"

"My mom was here this morning. She told me everything. If you talk to him again, please send him my gratitude."

"If I see him, I'll be sure to tell him."

"And Mom told me you two have patched things up."

"It was touch and go at first, but yes."

"Has Danny mentioned his little girlfriend, Lexie Turner?"

Lynn chuckled. "I think it's a mutual crush. She was beaming last week when Danny got on the school bus."

"Before we know it, he'll start dating." He leaned his head back and sighed. "I don't know if I'm ready for that."

"That makes two of us. It feels like yesterday we were bringing him home from the hospital."

"Where does the time go?"

"I'd give anything to cradle him in my arms again." She made the motion with a reminiscing smile, then she dropped her arms and pouted her lips in disappointment. "He's grown so much, if I tried that now, he'd break my back."

Drew laughed haltingly then winced again. "Don't make me laugh. It's painful."

"Forgive me. I should get going."

"What? Why?"

"I need to get to your mom's house. Danny is with her. She invited us to stay for dinner."

Drew smiled weakly. "I'm glad you're finally out of the Andrea doghouse."

"Hang in there, okay?" She stepped back from the bed.

"Wait." The heart monitor beeped louder. "What about Beth?" His hands started shaking again. "Where is she?"

"In jail, last I heard."

"Are you sure?" His good eye was wide with terror. "What if she got out? Made bail?" The monitor beeped frantically. "She might show up here...try to kill me again. I gotta know..." He sat upright. "Don't leave me—"

"Drew..." She grabbed his hands and held them tightly. "Relax. Beth can't hurt you anymore."

"She can. I know. She's evil," he screamed.

Two nurses rushed in. "You better go," one told her as the other made Drew lie back. "He'll be alright, it's just the paranoia...from all the heroin he'd been given."

She back-stepped out of the room, and even with the door closed, she could hear him screaming for help.

Shaken, she reached the Recovery exit in time to see Beth step in front of her, holding a hypodermic needle. Lynn froze, alarm seizing control of her lungs. She couldn't breathe. She couldn't scream. *This can't be real.*

With a malicious grin, Beth cried, "You're next."

Lynn's knees felt weak, her head dizzy as her eyes blurred the horrific image before her. She fell back against the wall, blinked. No Beth. No needle. *What the hell is wrong with me?* She inhaled a deep breath then pushed through the exit door. Drew was safe, but neither of them truly free of her treachery.

While she rushed back to the parking garage, she wondered how many other cases there were like

Drew's. Someone who worked hard to get clean only to have sobriety yanked away. If she hadn't hired Jake, Drew would have been killed. She remembered her words to him, that she'd thank Jake: "If I see him again..."

There'll be no 'ifs' about it.

Once she was in her car, she took the phone out of her purse and scrolled to Jake's number. Goose bumps overtook her body as she imagined his strong arms around her waist, his chiseled chest pressed against her, those soft lips and that dimpled smile, oh my.

This is it. Take the leap.

Chapter 20

J ake answered on the first ring. "Lynn, I didn't think I was going to hear from you again."

She started the car. "I would have called sooner, but it's been a zoo around here."

The phone switched to the hands-free mode. "Have you seen Drew?" His smooth voice emanated from the car's sound system.

She set her cell phone in the cup holder. "I just left the hospital. He wanted me to thank you for everything you did." She turned left out of the parking garage onto Beaumont Ave.

"I'm just glad we found him in time."

She appreciated Jake using the word *we*, like they were a team. "He should make a full recovery, but it might take him a while before he stops blaming himself for what happened."

"Thanks for calling me with the update."

"There's one more thing. Do you know where Beth Meyers is? He's terrified she might get out of jail, find him, and finish the job." She felt a chill. "The whole idea freaks me out, too."

"I assume she's still locked up. I'll check. Is that all?"

"Actually..." she cleared her throat, "I thought about what you said. You were right about me not being in the right headspace Friday night, but you were also wrong."

"Yeah? How's that?"

"I wanted to kiss you, not because I was sad and looking for comfort. I like you and I think we owe it to ourselves to see if our feelings can go somewhere."

"Ah, ha. Now you're getting down to the nitty-gritty. I was afraid this was strictly a business call."

She exhaled a breathy laugh. "So, we're going out then?"

"Like on a date?"

"You're all about specifics."

"Occupational hazard."

"Yes. A date. I want to continue what we started Friday. Is that specific enough?"

He laughed. "How about next Friday? I can pick you up at seven. We'll get dinner and then—"

"Don't you dare say a movie."

"Okay...I know. How about something a little different?"

"Different?" She stopped at a traffic light. "How different?"

"Axe throwing."

"You have to be joking."

"I know it's unconventional for a first date, but it's super fun and besides, I think you and I are past conventional."

She giggled as she pulled into Andrea's driveway. "Okay, dinner and axe throwing it is."

"See you Friday."

She ended the call then sat in her car, imagining how their date could end. The possibilities made her stomach cartwheel. A steamy kiss? The whole shebang? She remembered how her body tensed up moments before their *almost* kiss.

She had been with a couple of men since her divorce, but it was purely physical. She had needs, after all. But sex with feelings? She hadn't had that since Drew. Suddenly she went from feeling excited and eager to guilt-ridden and doubtful. As attracted as she was to Jake, and as much as she wanted him, it seemed weird...going to bed with the man she hired to find her ex-husband. It had to be wrong on some level. And what if things between them got serious? What would Drew think? What would Danny think?

Stop over thinking it. This date is happening.

She stepped out of the car and headed for Andrea's front door. She was about to knock when the door swung open. Danny was standing there, wearing a big grin, with Snowball at his heels.

"Mommy." He jumped into her arms and gave her a big hug. "Look, Grandma let Snowball come over."

"I see that." She patted the top of Snowball's head.

Andrea came out of the kitchen with a blue and white dish towel slung over her shoulder. "Hi, Lynn. Dinner should be ready in twenty. We're having breaded chicken with sweet potatoes and veggies."

"That sounds delicious."

Danny tugged on her arm. "Mommy, can me and Snowball play outside until dinner is ready?"

Andrea spoke up before Lynn could respond. "How about we all go to the backyard. You and I can sit on the patio while Danny runs around with the dog."

"I really do need to get off my feet."

Andrea opened the hall closet and took out a couple of balls and a bubble wand, then led everyone outside.

"So how did the visit go?" Andrea asked, once she and Lynn were sitting comfortably on the patio sofa.

"It was hard to see Drew like that, brought back

a lot of hard memories. I just wish he didn't blame himself for what happened."

Andrea nodded. "Being in the hospital after an overdose, he feels like he failed."

"But he didn't. He was drugged against his will. Now he's all freaked out that Beth might show up and kill him anyway."

"He just needs time to process everything that happened." Andrea put her hand on Lynn's arm. "And you. How are you doing?"

She remembered the terrifying hallucination she suffered earlier and decided to keep it to herself. "I'm fine."

"That's about as believable as Danny hating ice cream."

"No, really. I'll be okay."

"Seriously though, Lynn. Thank you for everything you did."

"I didn't do all that much. I just hired Jake." The corners of her mouth twitched slightly at the sound of his name. She hoped her reaction went unnoticed.

Andrea grinned. "So, you and the P.I. are on a first-name basis?"

"It's not what you think."

"You like him. I can tell from that smile you tried to conceal. Oh, and the fact that you're turning as red

Katelyn Marie Peterson

as a strawberry right now."

"I am?" Lynn placed her hands over her cheeks.

"I knew it," Andrea said triumphantly.

"Okay, fine. Yes, I like Jake, what I know about him anyway."

"And? Are you going to pursue him?"

"Andrea, maybe we shouldn't—"

"Oh, Lynn..." She huffed. "Stop playing coy with me. I know what it's like to be attracted to someone, to have urges. Sometimes you need to act on them."

Lynn scrunched up her nose. "Ugh, Andrea."

She scoffed. "What? You think I'm a nun?"

Lynn placed her hands over her ears. "La la la la. Sorry, I can't hear you."

Andrea spoke louder. "You know how to make me stop." She laughed. "Tell me what I want to know."

She brought her hands down from her ears. "If you insist on knowing, Jake asked me out and I said yes."

"Now, was that so hard?"

"Uh, yeah. Excruciating, in fact."

"Why?"

"For one thing, your Drew's mother. And for another, you just started to like me again. Talking about another man feels...awkward."

"News flash, Lynn. I always liked you. You deserve to be happy, even if it's not with Drew."

"Honestly, I've been feeling a little guilty about the whole thing with Jake."

"Not on my account, I hope."

"No, not you. Though your opinion matters." She sighed. "The entire time Jake was looking for Drew, I found myself becoming more and more enamored."

"And you think that's wrong?"

"Well, isn't it? How self-absorbed do I have to be?" She shook her head. "Danny and Drew would not approve. I've only known Jake for a week. I should cancel the date."

Andrea gasped. "Absolutely not. Lynn, you are being way too hard on yourself."

"Maybe."

"There's no time limit on falling in love. Honey, you always put other people first. Danny, Drew, your friends. It's about time you do something for yourself. Not that you need it, but if it will help, you have my blessing."

She started to tear up. "Thank you, Andrea. You have no idea how much that means to me."

Andrea leaned in for a hug. "So, you won't cancel the date?"

Lynn smiled. "If I fall in love, it's all your fault."

"Fair enough. Let's eat. Danny, dinner is ready."

"Yay, dinner." Danny and Snowball rushed into the house.

Lynn trailed behind, her mind wandering. She should have been mentally celebrating. Everyone was happy and safe, for the most part. And Andrea said some of the nicest things Lynn had ever heard from her. So, why was it so hard for her to relax?

Chapter 21

Lynn stood hunched over the bathroom sink at work and splashed water on her face. She was mentally exhausted. She'd spent the entire week going through a cycle of emotions. She'd start the day feeling excited about her upcoming date with Jake. Later, she'd find herself worrying about Drew, hoping that he'd overcome the setback Beth had laid on him.

Last night, she'd tossed and turned, suffering from fear induced flashbacks from that night at the metalworks. The hallucination at the hospital, with Beth blocking the exit and threatening her, didn't help matters. Then she'd come to work, and instead of feeling that usual rush of joy she got from her job, she felt bored. She'd gotten used to working with Jake on a day-to-day basis. Now she was in total withdrawal.

"You got this," she said to herself. "Just two more hours."

When she walked into her office, there was a big flat box on her desk. The poster for Violet Miller's mother, Lydia. She opened the box and carefully lifted out the laminated artwork. "Wow," she whispered. In the center of the poster was a current picture of Lydia with her family. She was in the middle and was wearing a blue short-sleeved dress with a string of pearls double-wrapped around her neck. The rest of the photos depicted Lydia's life from childhood to adolescence to early adulthood. In almost every photo, she was wearing blue: blue jeans at a family picnic, a strapless blue dress at her prom, and a blue skirt at a sorority function.

Lynn took out her phone and snapped a picture of the poster to send to Violet. A 'thank you' came back, followed by several smiling emojis.

Ten minutes later, her two o'clock appointment commenced. The potential client, Alice Moore, was looking to hire someone to plan her co-worker's retirement party. They worked at the same middle school for the past thirty years.

"So, Ms. Moore, tell me a little bit about your co-worker..." she glanced down at her notes, "Madeline."

Alice smiled. "Maddie loves her students. Working at that school wasn't just a paycheck for her. And the feeling was mutual. They all made cards for her, beautiful ones with the sweetest messages inside them."

"That's so thoughtful. And what about Maddie's

interests?" She felt like she was standing outside of her body, watching and listening as her boring conversation with Alice unfolded. Though she enjoyed learning about Maddie, a woman who wasn't just dedicated to her students but was also a volunteer reader at the children's hospital and a server at her local soup kitchen, all she could think about was how much she wanted to wrap up the meeting and call Jake. *Surely he must be working on a case more exciting than this.*

"I must admit, Ms. Callahan. I met with a few other event planners before I contacted you. While they were certainly qualified, you made quite an impression on me. I like the fact that you wanted to know so much about Maddie, which is why I would love for you to plan her retirement party."

"I'm happy to hear that. I'll start contacting venues, florists, and local DJs. In the meantime, do you think you could get your hands on those cards you were telling me about? I can use them as a decoration theme."

"Certainly." Alice stood from her chair. "It was very nice to meet you, Ms. Callahan." She extended her hand.

Lynn accepted the handshake. "Likewise, but please, call me Lynn."

Shortly after Alice left, Lynn took her purse off the door hook and walked out of her office. "Have a nice weekend, everyone." That was met with several smiles and goodbye waves.

"See you Monday," Angela said.

On the way to her car, she ran through a mental list of what she had to do: pack a night bag for Danny's overnighter at Melanie's, drive him over there, shower, and get dressed... She wondered if she would be ready in time to enjoy her date with Jake.

***

When Danny got home from school, Lynn greeted him with a big hug and kiss, inside the house, of course, so as not to embarrass him in front of his friends on the bus. "How was school, bud?"

"Good. Can we go see Daddy now?"

She sighed. "You're spending the night at Aunt Melanie's, remember?"

"Oh, yeah." Danny slapped his forehead. "Silly me. Is Snowball coming too?"

"Yup. He'll probably get spoiled with Aunt Melanie's homemade dog treats."

"Maybe we can see Daddy tomorrow."

"As soon as he gets home, honey." She walked into his room and opened the closet to take out his overnight bag and packed it with PJs, a fresh change of clothes, and his toothbrush.

"What about Oscar's birthday party tomorrow? We're still going, right?"

"His birthday present is in here." She tapped the overnight bag. "I think he's really going to like the action figure you picked out for him. Who was it again?"

He giggled. "Doctor Strange. From the movie. Remember?"

"Now I do." She smiled. "Okay, bud, let's go."

He scooped up Snowball in his arms and ran out the door in front of her.

***

When she got home from dropping Danny off at Melanie's, she rushed through a shower then rifled through her closet and drawers. She needed an outfit that was comfortable enough for axe throwing but still made her feel sexy. She decided on dark blue jeans and a fitted white V-neck with three-quarter sleeves. To accompany the outfit, she chose a pair of small silver hoop earrings and a silver heart necklace.

Once she was dressed, she walked into the bathroom and opened the middle drawer of the vanity where she kept her makeup bag. She was never heavy-handed with her makeup: a swipe of brown eye shadow, a light drawing of black eye liner, and pink lipstick did the trick.

As a final touch, she applied two sprays of perfume around her neck. Pleased with the floral scent of lavender, jasmine, and vanilla, she placed the bottle back in its drawer and walked into her garage to get a pair of sneakers off the shoe rack. The doorbell rang just as she was coming back into the house.

When she opened the door, Jake's eyes widened, and his jaw dropped a little. "Wow." He smiled, displaying those dimples that first drew her in.

"I'll take that as a compliment." She laughed.

"You're stunning, absolutely stunning."

"You look pretty 'wow' yourself."

Jake's black pants and red flannel shirt, open down the front, with a white t-shirt underneath, complemented his lumberjack look nicely.

She grabbed her purse and locked up. "What did you find out about Beth?" she asked as they walked to his car.

"She's still in jail, can't hurt you or Drew, but forget about her tonight. I was thinking we could go to the Farmhouse Tap and Grill downtown."

"I haven't been there, but I love good bar food."

"It's not far from BurlyAxe Throwing on Winooski." He opened the passenger door, and she got in. When he got in behind the wheel, he looked over at her. "I'm really glad you called me." Then he moved in a bit to brush a few strands of hair from her face. He set his hand against her cheek while he gazed into her eyes before pulling away to start the car.

She was expecting nervous butterflies to surface in her stomach or her heart to start racing, but nothing like this flood of desire.

Call 911.

Chapter 22

Lynn was surprised at how quickly they were seated at Farmhouse, given how lively it was inside.

"Lacey will be with you shortly." The hostess placed two menus on the table.

Lynn glanced around the room. The restaurant was large and brightly lit, with almost every table and booth occupied. There were a few couples, some families, and some solo customers. The spacious outside patio was just as crowded.

For a restaurant this popular, she was expecting the noise level to be overwhelming, but the chatter was low, musical even. The décor matched the cozy ambience with strategically placed hanging lights and a small table lamp at every booth. A three-sectioned chalkboard above the bar touted their drink menus in handwritten white chalk.

"I guess you've eaten here before." She looked over the menu.

"You could say I'm a regular. I usually come here with my friends from the police department."

"Lucky me, then."

Jake laughed. "I'd say it's the other way around." He leaned forward. "By the way, you smell amazing." He'd said that just above a whisper, then he took her hand in his and stroked it tenderly with his thumb, sending a shiver up her spine.

Their waitress came up, breaking the sensual silence. "I'm so sorry for the wait. May I start you off with a couple of drinks?"

Jake let go of her hand and sat back. "Lynn?"

"I'll have the raspberry lemonade, please."

"Pepsi for me."

"I'll be right back with those drinks."

"Do you know what you want to eat?" he asked. "My favorite thing here is the Angus Farm beef burger with onion rings."

"Oh, onion rings. I could go for those, but instead of the beef burger, I'd like the Stonewood Farm turkey burger. The grilled apples that come with it sound delicious."

Lacey came back with their drinks and took their orders: the beef burger for Jake and the turkey burger for Lynn, both with onion rings. "Okay, I'll put that order in right away."

Lynn watched Lacey saunter off then turned her attention back to Jake. "This is usually the part of the evening where we get to know each other a little better."

"What do you want to know?"

"Hmm." She tapped her chin. "Name the craziest thing you've ever done."

He smiled. "That's easy. Skydiving."

She widened her eyes. "Really? You don't strike me as the jumping-out-of-a-plane type."

"I'm not." He chuckled. "My girlfriend at the time convinced me to go, said it'd be a fun adventure."

"Ah. And it wasn't?"

"It was fun but definitely not something I'd do again."

"The relationship must have been pretty serious if you were willing to jump out of a plane for her."

"It was. At the time. Dana and I dated for two years. We met through a mutual friend and moved in together after six months. That was four years ago."

Dana. Pretty name.

Lynn was relieved when their waitress came with their food, an intermission for her curiosity. She took a bite of her turkey burger. Determined to learn more about Dana, Lynn pressed ahead. "So, umm, what happened between the two of you?"

"A few months after our two-year anniversary, I

woke up to a note on my nightstand, and all of her things were gone."

Her jaw dropped. "She Dear John'd you?"

Jake laughed a little. "I never thought of it that way, but yes."

"Did she say why she left?"

He swallowed then took a sip of his Pepsi. "My job was the biggest reason. She said I worked too much, that she was tired of going to bed at night and worrying about my safety."

"That must have been hard for you."

"I was hurt and angry for a while, trying to make sense of it all, but in the end, I realized she did us both a favor."

Lynn dunked an onion ring in ketchup. "How so?"

"We had very different personalities. I'm an organized person, a little reserved, maybe a little anal retentive. Dana was the far opposite...carefree, spontaneous, and expressive with her emotions to a fault."

"Opposites attract, right?"

"High maintenance. She made the relationship exciting, which is probably why I chose to ignore a couple red flags."

"Like what?"

"Like the fact that she didn't want kids, or that she scoffed at the word *marriage.*"

"Those are pretty big differences."

"I have no regrets about Dana. We weren't right for each other." He reached for his napkin. "Things happen for a reason, right?"

"We certainly wouldn't be here tonight if she hadn't left you."

"My point." He finished the last bite of his burger. "So, you ready for the next part of our date?"

She chuckled nervously. "Were you ready to jump out of a plane?"

He laughed. "You're going to like it. Trust me."

Trust was easy with Jake. But axe throwing? She still had her doubts.

I guess I can't knock it until I've tried it.

Chapter 23

Lynn wasn't sure what to expect when she walked through the front entrance of BurlyAxe Throwing. Never had she imagined herself throwing an axe for any reason, let alone doing it on a first date.

The inside of the center was welcoming. It was a large bright room divided into several lanes with high chain link fencing, most of them already occupied. There were high tables and stools set about. The thumping of axes striking wood and cheers from onlookers filled the air as competitors hit their targets. The scent of pine and sawdust appealed to her, earthy like Jake.

Maybe this won't be so bad.

A burly man with a thick beard and brown eyes greeted them at the counter. He was wearing a dark green shirt with a name tag that read *Shayne*. On the wall behind him hung several rows of short-handled axes. "Have you been here before?"

"I have," Jake said. "I booked an hour session."

He checked his monitor. "Jake Connolly. Okay, so

you know the routine." Shayne looked at Lynn. "Is this your first time?"

She glanced around the room. "I feel so out of place."

"Don't sweat it," Shayne said. "You'll have a blast. I'll just need you to read and sign this liability waiver." He handed them a sheet of paper and a pen.

"What are you getting me into?" she whispered.

"It's just procedure. Everything will be fine."

"Says the person who's actually thrown an axe before."

Shayne belly-laughed. "I'll coach you, show you what to do, step by step."

"And..." Jake added with an elbow nudge to her arm, "I'll be right there with you."

"We should have gone to a movie." She signed her name and handed the waiver back to Shayne.

"That'll be twenty-seven bucks apiece."

Jake handed him a credit card. "See. It's just as expensive as a movie."

She laughed.

"Okay, folks, you'll be in lane six." He took two axes off their wall hooks and led the way to a dark galley of double lanes with brightly lit targets downrange.

Why did I agree to this?

Led by Her Heart

When they reached lane six, Shayne looked at Lynn. "The way we do things, I show you two different throwing styles, then you repeat them and retrieve the axes."

Shayne stepped up to the thick black throw-line. "We'll start with the two-handed throw. You want to pick up the axe with your dominant hand. Mine is my right. And you want to have a firm grip around the base of the handle." He placed his left foot forward.

She studied Shayne's movements carefully. He stretched his dominant arm out in front of him at a forty-five degree angle, with his fist pointed toward the target. Then he wrapped his other hand around the hand that was holding the axe. "Now, I'm going to draw the axe back over my head and breathe in as I transfer my weight to my back foot."

He puffed his chest as he breathed out and moved his body and the axe toward the target. Then he shifted his weight to his front foot and released the axe at the wood-planked target. The axe blade cut into the bullseye.

"Now I'll demonstrate the one-handed throw, but for a beginner such as yourself, I recommend using the two-handed method."

Once Shayne was done with the demonstration, he looked at Lynn and smiled. "Okay, newbie. You're up."

Jake ran down-lane and retrieved the axes from the target, handed one of them to Lynn, and placed the other in a wooden box between their lanes.

She placed the axe in her right hand, her sweaty palms greeting its smooth base.

Please don't let me make a fool of myself.

She stepped to the throw-line and took a deep breath, then she slowly executed the steps she memorized from Shayne's demonstration. Her stomach flip-flopped as she watched the axe leave her hand, barely grazing the target before it dropped to the floor with a loud thud. Her cheeks warmed with embarrassment.

So much for not making a fool of myself.

"Not a bad start," Shayne said.

"Really? We must be seeing different targets."

Shayne laughed. "Have you ever played basketball?"

"Umm, yeah. I wasn't any good at that, either."

"You flicked your wrist like you were throwing at a basketball hoop. Let's try it again...and keep those wrists straight."

She ran to the target, picked up the axe from the floor, and walked back to the throw-line. In spite of all the axes flying by her on either side, the high chain-link fencing offered a reassurance of safety. Back at the throw line, she threw the axe again. This time the blade dug into the wood below the bullseye and off to the right.

Shayne and Jake clapped.

"Well done," Shayne said. "Now try the one-handed throw."

Lynn retrieved the second axe from the wooden box and stepped to the throw-line, but as she released the axe, she lost her balance, and the axe hit the floor under the target.

"Keep your eye on the target, not the axe. Try again."

Her brow started to sweat, and her knees locked up a bit.

I hit the target once. I can do it again.

Jake collected both axes, and she tried again. When the axe dug into the target below the bullseye and to the left, relief washed over her.

Jake ran down-lane to get her axe then came back for his turn at the throw-line.

Shayne turned to Jake. "Since you've done this before, this should be a breeze."

Jake stepped into position and lifted the axe over his head, wielding it like a Greek god. She watched the axe zoom through the air with grace and precision then dig into the bullseye.

"Impressive," Shayne said. "Now the one-handed throw."

Jake took the second axe out of the box. Once again, his strength dominated the axe, and it struck the target with authority. He hop-skipped in victory as he fetched the axes.

Who knew I could get turned on at an axe throwing center?

"Okay, folks, demonstration's over. Your hour starts now. Have fun."

Jake handed her an axe. "Ladies first. You ready?"

"Yeah," she said while shaking her head *no*.

Jake laughed. "You're going to like it. Trust me."

"If you say so." She stepped to her throw-line and replayed each step of the two-handed throw. The axe soared to the target boards and dug in just inches from the bullseye. She jumped with excitement and did a little dance. "Oh-yeah."

"Nice shot."

She watched Jake step up to the throw-line with the axe in his right hand. Then he turned slightly and smiled at her. "Remind me never to piss you off." This time his throw went wide right, and the axe clattered to the floor.

Led by Her Heart

"What's the matter, Jake? Did I rattle you a little."

"In more ways than you know."

"Oh?"

They walked to the targets to retrieve their axes.

"I have to admit..." She smiled slyly. "That felt good."

"Now you know why I like coming here. It's a great way to relieve stress."

She could think of another fun way to relieve stress, but she kept that thought to herself. Fifteen minutes into their session, Jake dropped his axe into the wooden box. "Let's take a break."

"Okay." She placed her axe next to his.

"Would you like some water?"

"Sure. Thanks." She sat on a stool at a high table.

He came back with two bottles of water, handed her one, then claimed the stool next to her. "So, what do you think?" He guzzled some water.

"I can't believe I'm actually here...doing this...let's get a picture." She slipped her phone out of her back pocket and leaned into him for a selfie with the BurlyAxe logo behind them.

Click.

She showed him the photo.

"Hey...we look good together."

"I think you're right."

"Can I hear that again?" He cupped a hand behind his ear. "The part about me being right."

She leaned in closer. "You're right," she said in a seductive whisper.

He stared into her eyes, studying them like they were rare and precious jewels. "I've been wanting to do something all night."

"Yeah? What would that be?" She gave him a knowing smile.

He extended his hand to the back of her head and brought her lips to his for a slow, sweet kiss. Then she took the reins by parting his lips with her tongue. He responded with more pressure on her mouth, more breathing, and pulled her closer to him.

She placed her hand on his knee and closed her eyes while their tongues played a game of touch and taste. It was a kiss well worth waiting for. To come up for air, she pulled out of the kiss, opened her eyes, and saw axe-wielding people gawking at them. She'd forgotten they were in a public place, pitched them a sly smile, and they went back to minding their own business.

Jake was rubbing her back. "You sure have a way with folks."

"It's the party planner in me," she said breathlessly. "What else should I know about you?"

"I'm training for the Vermont City Marathon in May. I ran track in high school and college, kept up with it since. Running is cathartic for me."

"Like axe throwing?"

"Every bit of it helps."

"I guess you need that in your line of work."

He leaned in to kiss her again, but she put her hand to his chest to stop him. "We only have thirty minutes left of our hour. You certainly don't want to waste it kissing me."

"Sign me up for another hour." He kissed her anyway and then stepped down from the stool.

Licking her heated lips, she returned to her place on the throw-line. Axe in both hands, she found it hard to focus on the target. That kiss had started something she wanted to finish properly.

***

When they got back to her house, he resumed from where they had left off, pressing her against the closed front door, kissing her with a passion she'd so wanted to share with him.

She guided his hand up the back of her blouse, hoping he'd get the hint. He caressed her back, teasingly, then he worked his fingers up to the clasps on her bra, which he deftly unclasped. The relief on her chest was both welcomed and exciting. She became a sweet onion, slowly being peeled as he slipped her blouse over her head and the bra straps from her shoulders. His hands were roaming, and her heart was racing while every other part of her was heating up for the man she'd fantasized about.

He lifted her up, and she wrapped her legs around his waist. The kissing was hot and heavy as he carried her to her bedroom.

They were up against another closed door, this time with her at the helm. She unbuttoned his red flannel shirt and tossed it to the floor, then lifted his white t-shirt up over his head, and then she kissed every part of his chiseled chest.

At her command, he moved with her until they reached the foot of her bed. Then he took control, laid her down, and began kissing the round slopes of her chest, the nipples at their crests, and the valley between. She reached down and unbuckled his belt and zipped his zipper down.

At that, he stood, kicked off his shoes, and dropped his drawers.

She gazed at what his pants had been concealing. Reality was bigger than her wildest fantasies. She wriggled out of her jeans and panties, and soon their bodies became one, and the pleasure that ensued measured up to a sky full of fireworks.

Led by Her Heart

A few hours later, with Jake asleep in her bed, she carefully got up to use the bathroom. When she got back under her sheets, she found herself tossing and turning with a growing pit in her stomach.

Every time she closed her eyes, her hallucination at the hospital came back. Beth was standing across from her holding that damned hypodermic needle. "You're next," she kept saying with an evil grin. *Next? What poison was in that syringe? The irrational part of her took over. Heroin? Meth? GHB? LSD? Would she die of an overdose?*

Keep your guard up. Be prepared.

She had always been a worrywart. Becoming a mother amplified that. The minute she started to breathe easy, she was forced to put out another fire, whether at work or in her personal life. However, now her life was steady again, on track, better than good. Leave it to Beth to destroy it all...

Her rational voice piped up. *Drew is recovering. He'll be okay. Danny is happy. And Jake...* She lifted the sheet to admire his naked body.

He's here for me now. Just relax.

She wanted to listen to her rational self, but the worrying part of her was loud, overpowering, and quite annoying. One thing was for certain. She wouldn't be sleeping for the rest of the night.

Chapter 24

Lynn's eyes adjusted to the sunlight peeking through her bedroom curtains. She turned slowly to look at her alarm clock: *7:00 AM.*

Wow. I did fall asleep.

However, she didn't feel refreshed. She felt as if she'd been up all night, tossing and turning, warding off visions of Beth. She let out a big yawn and stretched her arms out slightly. As she started to get out of bed to make herself a cup of coffee, he woke up before her feet hit the floor.

"Good morning," he said with a sleepy smile.

She wriggled back under the sheets. "Last night was—"

"Incredible," Jake finished. He pulled her toward him and planted butterfly kisses on her neck. Then he stroked her bare thigh.

She let out a soft moan, then pulled back. "We don't have time for this. I need to pick up Danny, and you have to get to work."

"Not for another hour and a half." He ran his fingers through her hair while continuing to kiss her neck.

She pressed herself close to his chest. "Well...I didn't give Melanie an exact time." She kissed his cheek, then his lips.

"Then I say we go for round two."

"Round two coming up," she repeated softly.

He wrapped his arms around her waist and maneuvered her body over his.

This is way better than coffee.

***

Melanie opened the front door just as Lynn was getting out of her car. She had on her 'I Can't Bake Without Coffee' shirt and blue pajama shorts. "Good morning," she said in a sing-song voice. She had more energy than Lynn ever did on a Saturday morning.

Before Lynn could return the greeting, Melanie gasped and caused Lynn to stumble a little as she stepped through the front doorway. "Geez, Melanie, are you trying to give me a heart attack?"

"For someone who just had sex, you're a wee bit cranky." She laughed.

"Melanie, stop. Danny might hear you."

"Oh, relax. He's in the guest bedroom with Snowball." She grabbed her by the hand and took her to the kitchen then pointed to one of the chairs. "Sit."

She did as she was told and placed her keys and

purse on the table. Then Melanie sat in the chair next to her and scooted it close to hers. "Tell me everything."

"What makes you think there's anything to tell?"

"Call it a gift." She pointed her index finger at her. "Now spill."

"We went to dinner, and then we threw a couple of axes."

Melanie arched her eyebrow. "Is that a euphemism for sex? I thought I knew them all."

"No. We actually went axe throwing."

"Oh...that place..." She snapped her fingers. "BurlyAxe?"

"It was a lot more fun than I thought it'd be."

Melanie waved a dismissive hand. "Enough about the axe business. Get to the good stuff."

She knew what Melanie wanted to know, but she was having fun dragging it out. "By good stuff, I assume you mean... ah... what do you mean?"

"The sex. Tell me about the sex." Melanie's voice was ripe with impatient enthusiasm.

"Oh, that." She grinned.

"I knew it. How was it? Good? Great? Amazing? I bet it was amazing. He looks like he'd deliver well in bed."

Lynn had to laugh. "You're so bad. But you're

wrong. He pulled out, made a big mess, and cried for his mother."

Melanie stopped breathing. "No."

"I've never experienced anything like it."

She gasped. "You have got to be kidding me."

"I am."

"You are?"

"He was a perfect gentleman."

"Does he have a brother?"

Lynn laughed. "Actually, yes."

Melanie smiled slyly and tapped her chin. "Hmmm. The thoughts I'm having right now."

"Easy, girl. I don't know if he's single."

"Well, get on it. Find out."

Lynn frowned. "You've got to be kidding."

"I am."

"Oh... Touché."

"Seriously though, I'm happy for you, Lynn."

"Because I had sex?"

"No. Because of that." She pointed to the smile on Lynn's face. "I haven't seen you happy like this in a long time."

"The whole night was amazing, but between you and me, I was nervous that the date wasn't even going to happen."

Now Melanie frowned. "What do you mean?"

She sighed. "Things have been a little weird for me lately, especially at work. My office used to be my sanctuary, my happy place, but all week, I found myself watching the clock, counting the hours until I could go home."

"You don't want to be there anymore?"

"After working with Jake, planning parties feels so mundane."

"So, what? You want to sell your business?"

"No. Maybe. I don't know."

"Okay, Lynn, listen to me. First off, you are more than just a party planner. You take pride in what you do. You make these parties personal and memorable. You have a natural talent, but you've also been through something traumatic."

"I wasn't the one who was kidnapped and drugged."

"No, but you were the one holding down the fort with Danny. Managing his fears and your own. Then you finally found Drew. Seeing him like that, it would mess anybody up."

"Yeah. I guess you're right. When I was visiting Drew, he'd had an episode...went crazy with fear that Beth would find him and kill him. Freaked me out so bad, when I was leaving Recovery, I thought I saw her coming after me."

Melanie placed her hand over Lynn's. "That must have been terrifying."

"The hallucination looked so real."

"Don't give up on your business. You need to give yourself time to heal before you make any life-altering decisions. And I know just the medicine you need."

"What's that?"

"A girls' night out with me, Lisa, and Valerie."

"We never did reschedule."

"We did not. So?"

"My schedule is kind of hectic right now, especially with Drew in treatment at River Rock. How about after he's completed the program?"

"That's a good idea. I'll text Lisa and Valerie to be on call. Meanwhile, what do you and Danny have planned for today? You're welcome to stay for lunch."

"I'm taking him to a birthday party for his friend Oscar."

"That's sweet. Maybe you'll drum up some business while you're there. Be inspired."

Her heart wasn't feeling Melanie's enthusiasm.

Chapter 25

Lynn and Danny sat in the car, their heads cocked to the side, their mouths open, and their eyes wide as they gaped at the house in front of them, a beautiful brick colonial with four white pillars surrounding the front porch. Three semicircular steps dropped to a plush green lawn.

"Wow," Danny said. "This house is huge."

"I can't imagine having to clean it, bud."

"I wish Snowball could see it. Sucks he couldn't come."

"Daniel Callahan. Your dad and I did not raise you to talk like that. Now come on. Make sure to take the present." She took her purse off the passenger seat and got out.

On the spacious porch, she rang the doorbell, which played a tune just as big and fancy as the house, but two beckoning refrains went unanswered.

"They're probably out back." She led the way to the white fence guarding the backyard.

Oscar's mom, Allison, waved to them from a second-floor wraparound deck. She walked quickly but gracefully down the steps to greet them.

One look at Allison in a butterfly printed sundress and white high heels made Lynn feel underdressed in her pink and white striped t-shirt with white capri pants and pink flats. Then she glanced at some of the other moms up on the deck, all in skirts or dresses, and she felt out of place.

"I'm so happy you guys could make it." Allison looked down at Danny and gestured to the present in his hands. "I'll take that, honey. Go have fun. There's a bounce house, arts and crafts table, and a face-painting booth."

"Yay." Danny ran off.

Lynn followed Allison up the steps to the deck where the gaggle of moms had gathered.

"If you're hungry, there are snacks inside on the kitchen table, and drinks are in the cooler by the door."

She was left to her own devices while Allison resumed her responsibilities as hostess. Surveying the deck, she recognized a few of the moms engaged in conversation. No one seemed to notice her standing there like an awkward statue.

I need food.

She opened the sliding door, and in the kitchen, took a paper plate off the table. She heaped a bunch of finger foods onto it, a few mozzarella sticks, some popcorn chicken, and a couple of fruit kabobs, then walked back onto the deck.

As she stood at the banister, munching on a mozzarella stick, one of the moms came up to her. She wore a green skirt and white blouse. On her feet, tan heels looked to be four inches tall. "You're Danny's mom, right?"

"Lynn Callahan." She offered her hand.

The woman accepted the handshake. "I'm Mallory, Lexie Turner's mom."

"Oh, yes. Danny talks about her a lot."

"Lexie adores him. I think they have a little crush going on there."

"It's nice to finally meet you."

"He mentioned to her that you're a party planner. He says you plan the 'best parties ever.'"

Lynn laughed. "My littlest fan."

"The reason I'm bringing it up is because my husband's birthday is in a few months, the big four-zero. I want to throw a party, make the day special. Do you have a card on you?"

"I do." Lynn placed her plate on the railing, then reached into one of the zipper compartments in her purse and pulled out a business card: glossy white with colorful balloons on every corner and her name and phone number embossed in the center. "My e-mail, website, and social media links are on the back."

Mallory took the card. "Thank you so much. I'll be in touch."

"Mallory," a voice called out.

She smirked a little. "Imagine that. I'm being summoned." She turned her attention to the bottom step of the deck where another mom stood.

Melanie was right. Lynn had gained a potential client and based on her observations, Mallory was chatty and well-liked, two qualities that boded well for client expansion. However, given Lynn's current state of mind, she wasn't sure that more business was what she wanted.

I better get my act together. And soon.

Chapter 26

Three weeks later, Lynn picked up her *Best Mom Ever* mug and took a big slow sip of her morning coffee. "Ahh. So good."

"What's good?" Danny asked from the living room, his eyes shifting from the TV to her.

She chuckled softly. "I was talking to my coffee."

"Oh." Danny turned his gaze back to the screen.

How quickly he found no problem with me talking to my coffee.

After she took the last sip, she stared into the empty mug. Usually a one-cup-a-day gal, today she was tempted to forgo her routine.

Screw the routine. Mama needs caffeine.

Drew was finished with his treatment at River Rock, and tonight was girls' night out while Danny stayed with his dad. She stood from her chair and walked to the coffeemaker on the counter.

Since attending Oscar's birthday party with Danny, she'd gained three new clients, on top of the two she already had in progress, Violet Miller and Alice Moore. She felt like an overworked zombie. On top of that, Danny had spent almost every day asking about Drew. 'When can I see him? Why do I have to wait so long? Isn't he better yet?' Without going into too much detail about his recovery process at River Rock, she'd said, 'Daddy is doing better but he wants to be one hundred percent when he sees you.'

As tired as she was, her creative juices were flowing, but the joy and passion for her career lacked enthusiasm. Excitement and a greater purpose were missing in her life. Jake would talk about his cases, but she felt left out of the action. So lately, she'd been playing with the idea of asking him to let her help with his investigations.

She poured her second cup of coffee, then returned to the kitchen table, thinking back to when she hired Jake to find Drew. She'd done her research on private investigators, knew their responsibilities and the impact they had on their clients.

The more she thought about it, the more it made sense. Becoming a private investigator could give her the fulfillment she was looking for, but the process was very involved and would require most of her focus. If she wanted to pursue investigative work, she'd have to sacrifice her business, something she'd poured her blood, sweat, and tears into. She wasn't sure if she was ready or willing to give up such a big part of her life to start a new career.

Danny's sudden presence in the kitchen broke her concentration. "Mommy, are you done talking to your coffee yet?"

"Almost, honey."

"How much do you have left in there?" He walked closer and peered into her coffee mug. "Oh, good. Not much. Hurry up."

She laughed. "Why the rush, bud?"

He looked at her wide-eyed. "Did you forget about Daddy?"

"Honey, it's only ten-thirty. He's not expecting us until noon."

"How long is that?"

"An hour and a half, but we'll leave sooner to get there on time."

"How soon?" He put his hands on his hips.

Lynn pointed to the oven's digital clock. "When you see the number eleven followed by a four and five."

His jaw dropped. "But that's forever." He hung his head low.

She took her last sip of coffee. "I have an idea."

He looked up expectantly.

"Would you like to go to the playground for a little while? We can go to the park near your dad's apartment building."

"Yay." He started jumping up and down, then stopped to give her a hug. "You're the best, Mommy."

"I try, bud." She gave him a kiss on the cheek. "Alright, let's go get dressed."

***

The playground distracted Danny for all of twenty minutes. He climbed the monkey bars a few times and slid down the slide twice. Then he swung on the swings for a few minutes and jumped off, landing on the grass in a superhero-like pose, after which, he ran back to her. "Is it time to go?"

That was a first. Danny loved the park almost as much as he loved playing with Snowball. If he had it his way, he'd live there, wild animals be dammed.

She took her phone out to look at the time. It was only eleven-thirty, but she was out of distractions. "I'll text Daddy to let him know we're on our way."

They arrived at Drew's apartment building ten minutes later. The moment they got out of the car, Danny started to run toward the entrance, not paying attention to his surroundings.

"Danny," she screamed, grabbed his arm, and pulled him back as a car passed by. "Never do that again."

"Okay. I'm sorry."

"You need to be careful." Heart hammering, she held his hand until they were on the elevator.

When they reached Drew's floor, Danny got off the elevator and ran down the hallway. Drew hadn't opened the door halfway, when Danny pushed through it and wrapped his arms tightly around his dad's waist.

"Hey, buddy." Drew returned the embrace and kissed the top of his head.

Lynn watched the tender moment from the doorway.

"I missed you, Daddy," Danny said into Drew's red t-shirt.

"I missed you too...so much."

When Danny finally pulled away, there was a cluster of tears in the center of Drew's shirt.

"Okay, buddy, let's move into the living room so your mom can get out of the hallway."

"It's okay," she said, her eyes burning with tears. "That hug was long overdue."

"I didn't think I'd ever see him again."

"So, how does it feel to be done with River Rock?"

He looked down at Danny. "Hey, buddy, go play in your room for a little bit while your mom and I talk."

"I never get to hear anything."

"Go."

Once Danny was out of the room, Drew took a seat on the couch and motioned for her to join him. "I'm taking things one day at a time."

"And what about...ah, never mind."

"It's okay, Lynn. You can ask."

"What's going on with Beth?"

"She's been charged with first-degree kidnapping and first-degree aggravated assault. The judge denied her bail because she swore revenge on both of us."

"Are you holding up alright? No more panic attacks?"

Drew sighed. "After everything Beth put me through, I realized I never knew what she was capable of. I'm relieved to know that she'll be locked up until her trial. So yes, I'm not worried about her being a threat...unless she beats the rap."

"She couldn't possibly have a defense."

"Her daddy's got money. Who knows what shyster lawyer he'll hire. I'm just sorry you had to go through any of this."

"I survived." *And met Jake.*

"I've been thinking a lot about Dale. What he was feeling when he reached out to me." He lowered his eyes like he was ashamed. "How I let him down."

"You're still blaming yourself?"

Drew looked up and shook his head. "If Dale did try to commit suicide, he was in a dark place after he contacted me. I've been thinking about going to visit him."

She frowned. "He's in a coma."

"I just want him to know he's not alone."

"He won't even know you're there."

"But I will. Besides, I read that it's possible for comatose patients to register things like the sound of someone's voice."

"You're a good man." She gave him a hug then rose from the couch and walked toward the hallway that led to Danny's room. "Danny, honey. I'm ready to leave."

He ran out and gave her a big squeeze. "Bye, Mommy."

"Have fun with your dad. I'll see you tomorrow."

Drew walked her to the door. "In case I haven't said it enough, thank you."

"No thanks necessary. I'll always be here for you."

Once she was inside her car, her attention was called to the unmistakable sound of an Amber Alert on her phone. A seven-year-old boy had gone missing that morning.

The alert included a photo that could have been Danny: same age, same height, similar hair and eye color. She shook her head and sighed. "That poor family." The Amber Alert cemented her earlier contemplations. She wanted to make a difference. She needed professional fulfillment. Being a private investigator would give her everything she'd been longing for.

No more questions. No more doubts.

Chapter 27

Lynn stood in her bedroom in front of her open closet with Snowball panting beside her right foot. She knew Melanie was planning to wear a dress, accompanied by very high heels. But Lynn was always partial to jeans over dresses unless the occasion called for formal wear. Tonight would be far from formal.

She took her navy hip-hugger jeans off the hanger, then browsed through her tops until she came to her red crisscross halter. Her leather jacket would pair well with the outfit. She tied it together with her short black boots that had silver studs on each side.

In two hours, at ten o'clock sharp, she'd pick up Melanie, so she took her phone off the kitchen counter and retreated to the living room.

Sitting comfortably on the couch, with Snowball beside her, she pulled up Jake's name in her phone and typed a text message: *'Can you meet me for breakfast tomorrow?'* She figured sharing big news—like wanting to become a private investigator—was better said in person rather than on the phone, especially since she planned on asking for his help.

'Love to. Where?'

'How about The Spot, on Shelburne? 8:00?'

'See you there.'

She placed her phone on the coffee table, then picked up the TV remote and clicked on her Hulu account. She was in the mood to watch a rom-com, and the first one that came to mind was Dog Days. She had watched it several times, not only for the cute story and recognizable actors, but because she loved watching it with Snowball. His reaction to on-screen animals always made her smile.

Sure enough, a few minutes into the movie, Snowball jumped off the couch and got as close to the TV as possible. His tail was wagging, and he was barking with excitement as the human characters interacted with their dogs. It was a great start to a fun night.

***

When Lynn arrived to pick up Melanie, she was on her front porch, sitting in one of her white rocking chairs. As predicted, she wore a knee-high black dress with flutter cap sleeves, a deep V neckline, and a ruffled hem. Around her shoulders, she had draped a black shawl, and to match it all, she had on peep-toe stiletto heels.

"How can you possibly walk in those stilts?" Lynn asked her when she got in the car.

"Very carefully."

"Asked and answered." She put the car in reverse, backed out of the driveway, and headed in the direction of JP's Pub, a dive bar with a great karaoke crowd, just ten minutes from Melanie's house. When she found a place to park on Main, she fed the meter, and then they walked a half block to the rustic brick building where Lisa and Valerie were standing out front. The amber glow of the lampposts gave shimmering highlights to Valerie's dark hair.

They waved as she and Melanie got closer. Standing side by side, they were complete opposites. Valerie Brown stood at five-foot-two, with a black pixie cut and blue eyes. Lisa Cooper was five inches taller with straight blond hair and green eyes.

Even their outfits were contradictory. Lisa wore a short-sleeved green dress with a brown corduroy jacket and black flats, while her counterpart had on a blue jumpsuit with a white denim jacket and white heels.

Appearances aside, their personalities were almost identical. They were very sweet and easy going, and almost always in a happy mood.

"It feels like forever since we've seen you guys."

Valerie gushed and started a group hug.

"Make way for me," Lisa said.

Lynn and Valerie opened their arms to let her in. Little girl giggles and pretty girl kisses went all around before they broke apart and turned to the entrance.

Melanie led the way inside. The dimly lit pub was filled with applause as two patrons stepped up to the karaoke stage. The overall atmosphere was cheerful and inviting, from the rustic paneled walls decorated with neon signs to the hundred-year-old stained carpet on the floor. A Budweiser Racer 8 lamp hung over a mirrored bar, and from the ceiling, an oscillating fan stirred the smoke-free air.

"We're *so* doing a group song." Melanie rushed to the sign-up booth.

Lynn and the others found a table, which were abundant, as most patrons stood around with drinks in hand and drunkenly sang along.

A long-haired waitress wearing multiple Mardi Gras necklaces placed four drink menus on the table then scurried off.

Lynn, Lisa, and Valerie shimmied out of their jackets and hung them on the back of their chairs. Seated, they looked over the menus.

For a moment, Lynn's mind was held hostage by

the little boy in the Amber Alert, but Lisa's voice brought her back.

"I think I'm going to have a Sex on the Beach. What about you girls?"

"Beer and a shot," Melanie said as she joined them. "There's a two-hour wait for karaoke."

"Then shots all around," Valerie chimed in. "Patron Silver. That should get us wound up."

Lisa laughed. "You make a good pitch, but tequila makes my clothes fall off."

That got a laugh all around the table.

Melanie looked at Lynn. "What about you?"

She shrugged. "I'm driving."

"Have one drink early," Valerie said. "You'll be sober by closing time."

Melanie opened her mouth to say something but was cut off by the sudden appearance of a very good-looking guy. He was tall and muscular with sleeve tattoos and dark hair that enhanced his piercing blue eyes. Lynn knew there'd be a competition for his attention between Lisa and Melanie.

"I'm Travis. Are you ladies ready to order drinks?"

Lisa flashed him a flirtatious smile. "I'll have a Sex on the Beach. Want to join me?"

"Peachy." Travis smiled slyly but maintained a

professional attitude. "And you?" He was looking at Melanie.

"Boilermaker. Budweiser and Jim Beam. I like handling something strong." She smiled and gave him a wink.

Travis smirked but didn't engage.

Lynn was next to order. "Lemonade for me, please."

"Designated drivers drink free," he said and looked at Valerie. "What's your poison?"

"How about a double shot of Patron Silver with salt and lime?"

"You got it. I'll be right back."

A group of girls got onto the karaoke stage, one of them wearing a plastic tiara and a white t-shirt that said 'bride'. The rest of them wore pink t-shirts with the words 'bride squad' printed across them.

The familiar, upbeat sound of Sweet Caroline got everyone in the pub singing along with the off-tune bridal party.

"I love this song." Valerie started swaying back and forth.

When the song ended, drunken cheers erupted for the singers, then Lisa got the group's conversation back on track. "Okay, Lynn, catch us up. How is Drew doing?"

"He's hanging in there. One day at a time. Danny's sleeping over at his apartment tonight."

"He must be so excited to have his dad back," Valerie said.

"It was definitely an emotional reunion."

"And what about you? What's new in your life?" She grinned wickedly like she already knew the answer.

"Melanie told you guys about Jake, didn't she." Lynn glared at Melanie who returned a sheepish grin.

Lisa groaned. "She didn't give up any details, so we want to hear it from you...and don't leave anything out."

"Hold that thought." Melanie's eyes were focused on Travis, who was coming back with their drinks.

He delivered them one by one, leaving Melanie's beer and a shot for last. She made sure to graze his fingers when she reached for the glasses.

"Enjoy." He stepped away, unfazed by Melanie's obvious interest.

"Do you have a picture of Jake?" Valerie asked Lynn.

She took her phone out and pulled up the selfie she took at BurlyAxe.

"Aw. He's cute," Valerie said.

"Kudos to you, girl," came from Lisa.

Melanie dropped her shot glass into her draft beer and took a long pull while the others chatted, moving on from Lynn's life to Valerie's recent breakup with a guy that none of them approved of.

Melanie hit the table triumphally. "Finally."

Lynn nudged Melanie's side. "Not so loud."

"Sorry, but he wasn't good enough for our Valerie."

"It took me a while, but I finally saw him for who he was, a pompous jackass with no sense of humor." Valerie downed her shot of Patron Silver.

Travis came back. "Is there anything else I can get for you ladies?"

"We're good for now," Lynn said.

Valerie slammed her empty shot glass on the table. "I'll take another one of these."

"Careful," he said. "They're dangerous."

She batted her eyelashes at him. "I like living dangerously."

"I've heard that line before." And off he went.

"I know something he could do for me," Melanie said. "And it has zilch to do with booze."

The girls broke out in raucous laughter.

"You are so bad," Valerie said.

"What can I say? I know what I like."

"I'm sure he knows too," Lisa said. "It's not like you've been subtle."

"Says Ms. 'I'll have a Sex on the Beach.'" Melanie took a slug of her spiked beer. "I like being direct."

Lynn wrapped her arms around Melanie. "We wouldn't have you any other way."

The others applauded, and then their names were called to the stage. "Already?" Melanie stood from her chair. "Okay, ladies. Enough talking. Time to sing."

"What song did you pick?" Lisa asked as they followed behind her.

She turned around and smiled devilishly. "You'll know when the intro starts."

They took their positions on the stage. A fast-paced drum rhythm started, followed by a heavy bass beat, then came the lively guitar riff of *Footloose*.

"Sing along everyone," Melanie shouted to the crowd. She held the mic stand with both hands, and led with the first two lines: *"Been working so hard. I'm punching my card."* Lisa joined her at the mic, and they belted out the next two lines: *"Eight hours for what? Oh, tell me what I got."* They turned away to let Lynn step up to the mic. As she sang the lines: *"I've got this feeling. That time's been holding me down..."* she realized just how much she needed a night out with her friends. Valerie stepped up, and they both let 'er rip: *"I'll hit the ceiling. Or else I'll tear up this town."*

Lynn felt rejuvenated, ready to welcome tomorrow with fresh eyes and hopefully begin the next stage of her life. Ninety-nine percent ready. There was still a small part of her that wondered if she was making the right decision by giving up her business to pursue a new career. Tomorrow's breakfast date with Jake could very well be the turning point.

"So now I gotta cut loose. Footloose."

Chapter 28

L ynn and Jake walked hand in hand toward the front entrance of *The Spot*. The aroma of coffee and bacon in the air made her mouth water. Inside, the surfer-style restaurant was large and spacious, not to mention bright and welcoming.

A petite woman with short blond hair and hazelnut brown eyes greeted them with a big smile. She was standing behind a long wood countertop with a big yellow and orange surfboard hanging above her. "Welcome to The Spot. Just the two of you today?"

"Two," Lynn said.

The waitress pulled menus out from under the counter. "Follow me, please." She led them to a table at the back of the crowded restaurant and placed the menus down. "Can I start you two off with something to drink?"

"Coffee, please," Lynn said.

"Orange juice for me," Jake said.

"Coming right up."

He smacked his lips. "I'm in the mood for

chocolate chip pancakes, maple syrup, and a side of bacon."

Lynn admired the dozens of beach-themed photos on the walls. "I'm a breakfast sandwich girl. Bacon, egg, and cheese all the way."

He grinned. "At least you got the bacon part right. Pancakes, no contest."

"Says you."

"Agree to disagree then?"

"Deal."

The waitress brought their drinks. "Are you ready to order?"

"I am," Lynn said. "I'll have the Triple Crown with bacon."

She looked at Jake. "Sir?"

"Chocolate chip pancakes with bacon."

"It comes with a fruit bowl."

"I'll pass."

"Coming right up."

He watched her walk away then leaned toward Lynn. "So, how'd it go yesterday at Drew's place?"

"He was thrilled to have Danny come over."

"We got lucky on his case. Another hour, he may have been too far gone to save."

"That's partly why I wanted to meet with you this morning."

"If it's about the money—"

"No. Not at all."

He raised his eyebrows. "Then you're breaking up with me and going back to your ex?"

She laughed. "I have some big news. You're the first person I'm telling."

"I'm honored...I think."

"After helping you find Drew, I started to feel like something was missing in my life. Like I needed a change, but I wasn't completely sure of what I needed until I left Drew's apartment yesterday." She took a deep breath. "There was an Amber Alert for a seven-year-old boy. His picture looked so much like Danny. My heart ached for him and his parents, and then it hit me. I wanted to help, to become a private investigator like you. Make a difference in the world." She held her next breath and focused on Jake's startled gaze.

"Wow, Lynn, that's huge. But what does that mean for your business?"

"I'm going to sell it."

Jake scrunched his eyebrows together. "But you love your work...making people happy."

"That's true, but the work you do, the work we did together on Drew's case, it was much more satisfying than I expected. Now it feels like a calling."

Their breakfast orders arrived. "Is there anything else I can get for you?"

"We're good for now," Lynn said. "Thank you."

"Of course. Enjoy."

Lynn picked up her sandwich and bit into it. After washing it down with a sip of her coffee, she looked at Jake chewing a forkful of his pancake. "You think I'm crazy?"

He swallowed and looked down at his breakfast. "Chocolate chips. Whoever thought of putting them in pancakes was a genius."

"Jake. Did you hear me?"

"I would have never expected chocolate and maple syrup to taste so good together."

"Jake?"

"You know what else I never expected...that you'd do so well at throwing axes...you surprised me there, but I have to admit, this surprise is bigger than I could have ever expected.

"Now you're screwing with my head. What do you think?"

"I think you're amazing, and passionate, and more determined than anyone I've ever met. The way you handled Drew's disappearance, how you wouldn't let it go when the police didn't take you seriously. The P.I. world needs a Lynn Callahan."

She smiled. "You have no idea how much that means to me."

"But you haven't got a clue what you're getting into."

"I was hoping you'd help me with the process."

"Process? It's not like planning a party. Step A, venue, Step B, caterer, Step C, vendors." He dug into his pancakes. "No. Not like mixing chocolate and maple syrup. Not that simple."

"I won't be ready right away. My business needs to be taken care of first. Employees. Clients..."

"You don't want to move onto one thing before finishing the other."

"Exactly." Lynn took another bite of her sandwich. "I can do more for the world than plan parties."

"And I bet you will. After you sell your business, we'll look into it." He gave her a teasing smile.

"Great." Lynn chewed and swallowed her bacon, egg, and cheese delight. "What do you have planned for the rest of today?"

"I guess that depends on you." He grinned. "What time do you have to pick Danny up from Drew's?"

"Sometime before eleven."

He looked down at his watch, then looked back

up at her. "That leaves us two hours."

"What should we do?" She began to stroke his leg with her foot. "Two hours can go a long way."

"They certainly can," he said in a low voice. Then he leaned across the table and gave her a kiss. "Want to get out of here?"

She nodded. Her body ached for his, yearning for a repeat of their last bedroom frolic: toe curling, weak in the knees, mind blowing sex.

We need to leave before I take him on this table.

***

Later that day, after she and Danny got back from Drew's apartment, Lynn got out her laptop and made herself comfortable on the couch.

"What are you doing, Mommy?"

"Research, bud."

"Like for a project?"

"Exactly. I have a big project coming up, and I want to be prepared."

"Can I help?"

She smiled. "How about you pick out a book and come read next to me."

"Okay." He ran upstairs to his room, then came back down with a pile of books and dropped them onto the couch next to her. "I don't know which one to read first."

She giggled. "My little bookworm." Then she looked through the pile. "What about this one?" She pointed to a dinosaur book.

"Yeah. Good choice, Mommy." He took the other books and placed them on the floor, cuddled up next to her, and began reading. Snowball quickly joined the cuddle session, snuggling under Danny's arm.

Once everyone was settled, she opened her laptop and began searching for local appraisers and business brokers. The more reading she did, the more excited she became about her upcoming venture.

Chapter 29

Lynn spent the next two weeks running from task to task. When she wasn't sending e-mails or making phone calls for clients, she was gathering information for her meeting with the business appraiser.

At night, after she tucked Danny into bed, she stayed up late, reading and taking scrupulous notes from the private investigator handbooks she'd found and purchased online.

She was exhausted. When she'd wake up from the little sleep that she did get, her head would be pounding. But now it was Friday, finally. Lynn could go home, leave her work at work, and focus only on being a mom to Danny and a girlfriend to Jake.

She sent her last e-mail of the day, then she leaned back in her chair and exhaled deeply. "Yes." She closed up shop and walked out her office door. "Have a good weekend, everyone."

Her employees acknowledged her, except for Angela, who was sitting at her desk, staring at her computer screen with a frown across her face. "Hey,

Angela. Are you okay?"

"Oh, yeah. Sorry. See you Monday." Her smile looked forced, and her lips were pressed together.

"I can tell something is wrong. Talk to me."

"I don't want to overstep. I know you're my boss, but I also consider you a friend."

"So, something *is* bothering you then."

"I'm worried about you."

"About me?" Lynn pressed her hand flat against her chest. "Why?"

"You come in every day with bags under your eyes like you haven't slept. I catch you taking short naps in your office, which you have never done since I've known you. I fear you are working too hard."

"You know about my power naps?"

Angela scowled, she was that serious. "I'm hired to know everything that goes on around here."

"You can rest easy. Really. And, by the way, you didn't overstep. I consider you a friend, too."

"Our relationship is important to me. I don't want anything to go wrong."

"Shut your computer off and walk out with me."

Once outside, Lynn asked, "Do you have any fun plans for the weekend?"

"I'm taking the kids out for dinner tonight, then tomorrow I'm dropping them off at my mom's house.

She volunteered to watch them for the weekend."

Lynn let out a breathy laugh. "Can't pass up an opportunity like that."

"Exactly. What about you?"

"Jake is coming over tonight to have dinner with Danny and me. The rest of the weekend, we're just going to take it easy."

"Danny meeting the boyfriend. That's big."

"They've met once before. I introduced Jake as 'mommy's friend,' same as I will tonight, not that I think of him as just a friend. I care about him a lot. I think I'm even..." She closed her mouth before she said more than she was ready to say.

"Hey, I get it. I'm a single mom too, remember? You're being smart." Her phone started to ring from inside her purse. "And that's my cue to leave."

"Have a good weekend," Lynn said.

"You, too."

When she got in her car, she closed her eyes and massaged her temples. Physically exhausted and mentally worn out, she was tempted to call Jake and reschedule their plans.

Still, she was eager to see him, to hug him and kiss him when Danny wasn't looking... That settled it.

Come on, girl. Time to wake up.

Chapter 30

When she got home, she headed straight for her bedroom to change out of her work clothes, slip into a pair of comfortable jeans, and pull on a light purple V-neck.

Danny's school bus pulled up in front of the house. Snowball scampered to the front door, wagging his tail and barking excitedly. "Hold on, boy." She opened the door, and before she could stop him, Snowball ran out to greet Danny.

"Hey, bud," she said when he walked in holding his trusty dog. "How was school?"

He put Snowball down. "It was good."

"Good is good." She bent to give him a hug but stopped when she noticed grass stains on his shirt and the knees of his pants. "Whoa, dude." She pointed to his clothes. "What'd you do, roll around in a ditch?"

He laughed. "Lexie taught me how to do a cartwheel."

"That's all fine and dandy, but before you do anything else, go take a shower and change clothes."

"Aw. Can I do it after dinner?"

"I don't want you looking like this at the table."

"Fine." He stomped to the bathroom and shut the door hard. Snowball scampered after him to sit and wait in the hall.

When he was finished with his shower and dressed in clean clothes, he took a seat on the couch next to her. "What are we having for dinner?"

"Pizza and cheesy garlic bread from Marco's."

"Yay. Pizza." He kicked his legs in the air.

She picked up her phone from the coffee table and looked at the time: *4:15*. Jake was coming around five. "How about I order it right now?"

"Yay."

She opened the pizzeria's app on her phone and placed the order: one large pie, half cheese only, half with bacon and mushroom, and added a side of cheesy garlic bread. After checking the *Delivery* box, she closed the app. "Okay. Food has been ordered. It should be here at five, same time as Jake."

"He's the man that saved Daddy, right?"

"He sure is."

"I should say thank you."

She smiled with pride. "I think that's a great idea, bud."

Jake arrived ten minutes after the pizza was

delivered. Snowball was the first to greet him with tail wags and a few licks to his hand. His other hand was hidden behind his back. "Hey there, Snowball." He stroked the puppy with his free hand. Then he looked up at Lynn. "Sorry I'm a little late. I had to make a quick stop." When he revealed his hidden hand, he held a pastry box from Sweets All Around Café.

Danny ran up to greet Jake, but the box captured his attention. "Are there cookies in there?" he asked with wide eyes.

Jake chuckled. "Why don't you see for yourself." He opened the box to reveal an assortment of cookies: chocolate chip, M&M, and shortbread, along with a few brownies and eclairs.

"You didn't have to do that," Lynn said.

Danny took the box. "But we're glad you did." He started to walk to the kitchen, then he stopped and turned around to face Jake. "Thank you for finding my dad." With that said, he turned around and ran into the kitchen before Jake could respond.

"I guess I did good," Jake said to Lynn with a smile.

"You did, and you look very nice, by the way." She ran her hand over the sleeve of his white Oxford button-down.

"This old thing's been collecting dust in my

closet for a while. I never had a good reason to break it out." He winked at her. "Until now."

She gave him a quick kiss before they joined Danny at the kitchen table.

Eight slices of pizza and half of the bakery box goodies eaten, Lynn and Jake stood from their chairs to clear the table.

"Can we play some games?" Danny asked.

She sat down and looked at the digital clock on the stove: *7:00.* "Sure. But bedtime is at eight, whether we're done or not."

"I never get to stay up late."

"Rules are rules, mister." She got up and headed for the hall closet where she kept the board games, but when she reached the door, she suddenly felt lightheaded, grabbed onto the doorknob for support, but her knees buckled.

Jake bounded from his chair and caught her. "Lynn, hey. What's the matter?" He gently turned her around so she was facing him and examined her with concerned eyes. "Are you okay?"

"I just got up too fast."

"I don't think it's that simple. You look a little pale."

"I've been working a lot lately...is all."

"Maybe we should watch TV instead."

"Danny wants to play a game...we play a game. I just need some water."

"Okay. But I'll get the games. Tell me which ones."

"Trouble, Scrabble Junior, Chutes and Ladders."

"Okay. Go sit."

When she wobbled back into the kitchen, there was a glass of water on the table.

"I got that for you, Mommy."

"Aw, thank you, sweetie." She took a few sips.

"Which one are we playing first?" Jake set all three board games on the table.

"Trouble," Danny said.

"Trouble it is." Lynn blinked, still a bit woozy.

They played one round of each game before she called for cleanup.

"Aw, can we play one more game? Please?" Danny looked at her with puppy-dog eyes and a turned down lower lip.

She stayed strong. "Sorry, kiddo. It's time for bed."

He hung his head in defeat. "Fine."

Once the games were put away, she told Danny, "Get changed for bed. I'll be up in a minute to tuck you in."

Moping, Danny walked up to Jake and gave him

a hug. "Goodnight, Mister Jake."

He patted the boy's shoulder. "Goodnight, Danny. Thanks for letting me hang out with you and your mom."

"You're welcome." He lumbered upstairs.

"I got a hug," Jake said to Lynn. "That's got to be a good sign, right? He likes me."

She scoffed. "Just wait 'til he gets you wrapped around his little finger." She gave him a smooch. "Get comfortable on the couch. I'll be right back."

Danny was already in bed, under his covers when she walked into his room. Snowball had made a nest in the dirty clothes on the floor at the foot of the bed. "What are you doing in here, boy?"

He wagged his tail.

She picked him up, prepared to take him downstairs.

"Ah, Mommy, he likes my room better than his dog bed. Let him stay here with me. Please?"

"Oh, I guess so." She petted Snowball on the head and set him down, then walked to Danny's bedside and bent to give him a kiss on the forehead. "Goodnight, bud."

"See you in the morning, Mommy."

When she reached the door he called, "Mommy."

She turned around. "Yeah?"

"I really like your friend."

That was music to her ears. "Good. He likes you too." She turned off the light.

Back in the living room, "Looks like you have a fan," she said to Jake. She took a seat next to him on the couch.

"You saying I have a way with kids?"

"You'll make a great dad someday."

"He's a great kid. I don't know how you do it."

"You mean being a mom?"

"No. I mean, everything. You're raising Danny, you've built a successful business, and now you're venturing into a whole new career field. You're incredible." He placed his hand against her cheek and stroked it gently with his thumb.

His intense gaze hastened her heartbeat. He was staring at her like she was a masterpiece that he adored. "I love you, Lynn," he whispered.

Her eyes widened. Did she hear him right? Did he say the words she'd been too afraid to say herself?

Her shocked silence must've compelled him to explain. "I know we just started dating, so don't feel like you need to say it back. I just—"

"Jake. Shut up." She threw her arms around his neck. "I love you, too."

His mouth found hers. Their tongues met with

familiarity, and his hands roamed her body with purpose, causing her to moan and her muscles to tighten. Butterflies let loose, but a sudden feeling of nausea urged her to back out of his embrace.

"Are you okay?"

She breathed a guarded breath. "I don't know." Looking down, she wouldn't let his gaze see her suddenly troubled eyes. "I think that last slice of pizza isn't settling well." The stairs that led to the bathroom seemed a million miles away. "I need you to go before I embarrass myself."

He stood. "Alright. Why don't we do lunch on Monday?"

She needed to get him out of her house, quickly. "I'll order from Deep City and bring it to your office."

"That sounds great." He gave her a peck on the cheek. "You better lie down. You're looking a little pasty again."

As soon as he left, she raced to the bathroom and retched. At least she got sick after they'd professed their love for each other.

Vomit was a real mood killer, for sure.

Chapter 31

Monday morning, Lynn woke up feeling beat. She'd seen more of her toilet bowl than she had of Danny all weekend. She wouldn't consider concerned questions answered through the closed door as mother-son entertainment.

It's a new day. Stay still, stomach.

She got out of bed and slowly walked to the kitchen, where she prepared breakfast for her and Danny: cereal and a plate of mixed fruit for him, toast and a banana for her.

She'd only taken a few bites of toast and had eaten half of her banana before she ran to the bathroom to hug the porcelain throne.

She heard Danny's footsteps coming toward the bathroom. "Are you okay now, Mommy?"

"I'll be right out, honey. Go get ready for school." She heaved again, feeling stuck in a never-ending-vomit cycle.

"Mommy, you have been throwing up a lot."

"I know, bud. Looks like I caught a stomach bug that's going around. I'll feel better soon." She used the sides of the toilet bowl to lever herself up off her knees and flushed. Her throat hurting and her body weak, she leaned on the sink. "The school bus...you don't want to miss the school bus."

"Okay."

She washed her hands and face and brushed her teeth. When she came out of the bathroom, Danny called, "Mommy, hurry up. The bus is here. Come on."

"I'm coming." She walked as fast as her cramping stomach allowed.

Danny had his hand on the doorknob when Snowball raced toward him, barking and wagging his tail. "Sorry, boy. You can't come with me." He bent down and gave the pup a few pats on the head. "Stay here and take care of Mommy."

Outside, the school bus door was folded open. Raucous laughter and chatter spilled out from kids who had no idea how hard life could be. "Have a good day at school."

"Bye, Mommy." He bounded aboard. The door unfolded, closed, and the bus roared off.

She lumbered back inside and fell onto the couch. Something on Friday night's pizza must've been rotten. She made a mental note of everything she'd eaten over the weekend. Melanie's sweets couldn't possibly be to blame. Danny wasn't sick, and as far as she knew, Jake wasn't either. That could only mean one thing. *I'm pregnant. Oh, no. It can't be.*

She'd taken her birth control like clockwork, never missed a day. Or had she. She wasn't late for her monthly friend. Or was she. Facts and fiction blurred together.

She ran to her bedroom and took her phone off the charger then opened her calendar and gasped when she saw that she was one week late.

I can't be pregnant. Not now.

She sat on her bed and took a few deep breaths. There was only one way to know for sure. She got herself dressed in a matter of minutes: acid wash jeans, a loose purple t-shirt, and tan sandals.

Before she left, she took Snowball for a walk, which luckily for her, was completed quickly.

"I'll be back later, boy." She squatted and gently took the dog's face in her hands. "Wish me luck, Snowball."

On her way to the pharmacy for a pregnancy test, she called Angela. "I won't be coming into the office today. If anyone needs me, tell them they can reach me on my phone or by e-mail."

"Sure, no problem. What's going on?"

"I'm just not feeling well."

"I knew you were coming down with something, for sure. I hope you feel better soon."

"Thank you for holding down the fort."

Lynn was hoping for much more than to just 'feel better.' She was hoping she wouldn't need to see her OB anytime soon. She was hoping not to gain twenty pounds over the next nine months. She was hoping not to have mood swings or have cravings for food she hated. She was hoping to fail the biggest test of her life.

We're not ready. I'm not ready.

***

Lynn sat in her car, staring down at the pharmacy bag. The last time she'd taken a pregnancy test, she was excited and hopeful. She and Drew wanted to start a family. They'd made the decision together, she took the test with him by her side, and when it read 'positive,' they were both elated. That was then.

Now, the possibility of an unexpected pregnancy so soon into her relationship with Jake loomed over her, plaguing her with fear. She and Jake had only been dating for a month and a half. A pregnancy would put a lot of stress on their new relationship.

I can't take this test alone.

She reached into her purse and pulled out her

phone to call Melanie. "Hey. Are you busy right now?"

Melanie laughed. "Of course I'm busy. It's cookies and pastry Monday at Sweets All Around Café. Why do you ask?"

"Can I come...can we meet at your house?"

"You sound freaked out. What's wrong?"

"I-I don't know...not sure."

"Okay. Deep breaths. I'll be there in ten minutes."

"Don't hang up...please."

"Tell me what's going on."

"I-I think I'm pregnant."

"Well that's a fine how-do-you-do. Did you get a pregnancy test?"

"I just picked one up. I don't want to take it alone."

"I'm here for you. You know that."

"I'm scared, Melanie."

"Do you know who the father is?" She snickered.

"Very funny." But it did make her laugh.

"See you at the house."

When Lynn pulled into the driveway, Melanie opened the front door and rushed out to the car.

Lynn got out, pharmacy bag in hand.

"Come here." Melanie wrapped her in a tight

hug and stroked her hair.

"What am I going to do?" Lynn felt new tears burning in her eyes.

"First things first. The test." She looped her arm around her, and they made their way to Melanie's front door.

Inside, Lynn headed straight for the bathroom. At the doorway, she looked over her shoulder at Melanie. "Wish me luck."

She offered a small smile. "I'll be right here."

Lynn closed the door behind her and walked to the toilet. After closing the lid, she sat down, and with trembling hands, she opened the box to take out the collection cup and one of the two digital pregnancy tests. She placed them on the vanity counter, stood up, and lifted the toilet lid. *Here goes nothing.*

As she was filling the cup, she remembered how awkward the test process was when she took it the first time eight years ago. She was so excited. So hopeful...

When the cup was full, she placed it on the counter and took the pregnancy test out of its wrapper. Her stomach was in knots as she dipped the tip of the test into her collected sample. When the stop light began to flash, she lifted it out, replaced the cap, laid it flat on the counter, and washed her hands.

"You can come in now."

They stood side by side with Lynn gripping Melanie's hand, making it as sweaty as her own. When the countdown ended, they looked down and Lynn gasped. Her entire body started shaking, and a tightness grew in her throat, preventing her from speaking the words.

Melanie gently let go of Lynn's hand and threw the test in the trashcan. Then she extended her arms out. "Come here."

Lynn sobbed as Melanie embraced her then led her out of the bathroom. They walked to the kitchen arm in arm. Seated at the table, Melanie said, "You're pregnant."

"I can't believe it."

"It's not the end of the world. You're going to be okay." Melanie got a bottle of water from the fridge. "Drink this."

"I'm pregnant. Not thirsty."

"You're pregnant."

"I am. I'm pregnant." She laughed.

Melanie laughed too.

Lynn took a swig of water. "Holy Toledo. Jake is going to be a dad....he said someday...with the right woman...he wanted to be a dad."

"He can't do better than you."

"But it's only been a month and a half. We haven't talked about kids or the future. We're both organized. We like schedules and structure. This was not on our list of things to do."

"The baby doesn't care about any of that."

"I can't imagine how he'll react. Look at *me.*" She motioned to her sweaty palms, her hands still shaking. "I'm a wreck."

"He cares about you, right?"

"Yeah. He, uh, he told me he loved me last Friday."

Melanie slapped the table with excitement. "Lynn, you left out the most important detail. And he said it first?"

"Yes. I thought I was dreaming."

"Then you have nothing to worry about. If he meant it, he'll stand by you. There's no reason why you two shouldn't be happy."

"You're right." She inhaled deeply. "I'm seeing him for lunch today. I'll tell him then."

Chapter 32

Lynn set the to-go order from Deep City on the passenger seat and her purse on the floor. The smell of the roasted garlic aioli emanating from Jake's smoked brisket burger was making her stomach queasy.

Great. Aioli makes me nauseous. What's next? Melanie's peanut butter chocolate chip cookies? Heaven forbid.

She averted her eyes from the to-go bag and started the car.

I hope I can eat my BLT. No. Focus on something else.

She decided her best use of time during the drive to Jake's office was to rehearse how she would tell him the big news.

'Jake, do you remember Friday night when we were kissing on the couch and I pulled away? Well, funny story...'

Funny story? He's not going to a comedy club. Try again.

'Jake, we need to talk...'

Whoa. No. Not the 'we need to talk' approach. That'll

put him on guard for something bad.

'Jake, I have something important to tell you. I'm not exactly sure how to say it. I'm pregnant.'

As good as it's going to get.

She pulled into the parking lot across the street from Jake's Courthouse Plaza office and sat in her car, trying to ease the angst in her stomach. She looked down at the to-go bag on the passenger seat and gagged again.

Here's hoping Jake's reaction will ease my nausea.

She turned off the engine, took her purse and the bag of food, locked up and headed into the building. "You can do this," she whispered to herself as she rode the elevator to the third floor. "Just tell him outright and face whatever comes next."

When she walked into the office foyer, she was brought back to the first day they met here. She was nervous that day, scared for Drew, unsure of his fate, but meeting Jake changed everything. Just from that one introduction, she felt a sense of ease and hope, and every day since then, Jake's presence had a way of making her smile and making her feel safe.

Melanie is right. He'll stand by me.

She walked to the reception desk, her heart pounding and her feet questioning their destination.

"May I help you?" the receptionist asked.

"You probably don't remember me. My name is Lynn Callahan."

"Of course." The girl smiled. "Jake said you were coming. You can head right in."

When she walked in, Jake was on his office phone. She closed the door quietly.

"Thanks for the update." He hung up. "Hey, beautiful." He walked to her, wrapped his strong arms around her waist, and kissed her like he meant it.

"Let's start every day off with a kiss like that."

"Hmmm." He chuckled lightly. "That sounds like a proposal."

"Maybe." She held up the bag. "Hungry?"

"Starving. I cleared room on my desk." He took the bag from her. "Come on. I already got us a couple of bottled waters from the vending machine downstairs."

She took a seat opposite him and placed her purse at her feet. "Who was that on the phone?" She picked up a water bottle and took a sip, hoping it would stay down.

He unloaded the bag. "That was a buddy of mine at the DA's office. I'd asked him to call with an update on Beth's case."

Her heart jumped. "I hope she gets life without parole."

He swallowed a bite of his brisket burger. "She's been a troublemaker at the jail, picking fights with the inmates and guards, and swearing revenge on everyone who put her there."

Her heart started to pound, which didn't help her queasy stomach. "Should we be worried?"

"She's under a high security watch. Her first court appearance has been postponed until she can be escorted safely. But enough about Beth. How was your weekend with Danny?"

She had the perfect opportunity to tell him right then and there, to save herself from having to scarf down food that would only come back up. But one look into Jake's gorgeous brown eyes and his famous dimpled smile, made her lose her nerve. "We mostly stayed home." She forced herself to take a bite of her BLT. Her body begged her to spit it out. She coughed.

"Are you okay?"

"I must have taken too big of a bite." She looked down at her sandwich, then placed it on the wrapper it came in. "Jake, there's something I need to tell you."

He swallowed a bite of his brisket burger. "What's on your mind?"

"This morning I—" She lowered her head and took a nervous breath. *Rip off the Band-Aid.* She looked up. "Jake, I'm pregnant."

His eyes widened. He stared at her then blinked. "You know, life is full of surprises, like this burger. It's one damn good burger. I thought it would be greasier."

"Did you hear me? I'm pregnant."

He closed his mouth, swallowed hard, then: "And Beth, boy, she was a surprise we didn't see coming."

"Jake?"

"And you, wow, you are full of surprises."

"It's not like I planned to get pregnant. I'm on the pill."

"Guess it didn't work. That's another surprise."

"What are we going to do?"

He looked at his half-eaten burger. "You know what they say about eating an elephant?"

"An elephant?"

"One bite at a time."

"I'm talking about a baby here."

He put his burger down, stood from his desk chair, then got down on one knee in front of her. "We're having a baby." His smile went from ear to ear.

"You're not angry?"

"Are you kidding? This is fantastic. I meant it when I said I love you. And yeah, it's sudden, but we're in this together."

"We are." She breathed a sigh of relief. "Yes, we are."

"We'll figure it out, one bite at a time." He gathered her in close and gave her a heart-melting kiss.

"Hey, lady," the receptionist shouted. "You can't go in there."

"Like hell I can't." The door swung open, and a petite woman with olive skin and wavy brown hair stormed in. "Hello, Jake. It's been a long time." Her big brown eyes were full of menace.

"Well, what do you know?" He released Lynn from his embrace, his brows raised as he gazed into her eyes. "What did I tell you about life being full of surprises?"

"Who is she?"

He turned to the intrusive woman. "Dana. What are you doing here?"

Dana? 'Dear John' Dana? What does she want?

"We need to talk."

Oh, no. Not the 'we need to talk' line.

She looked at Lynn, frowned, then glared at Jake. "Now."

"You can't show up after four years, brush past my receptionist, and start making demands."

She switched the strap of her purse to her other

shoulder. "Jake, please." Her voice softened. "I wouldn't have come here if it wasn't important."

"I'm in the middle of something important." He looped an arm around Lynn's shoulders protectively.

Dana looked at her again, this time with pleading eyes. "I don't mean to be rude. I just need a few minutes to speak with Jake alone."

Lynn couldn't help feeling both sympathetic and curious. She turned her head slightly and looked up at Jake. "You should talk to her." She rose from the chair and picked up her purse.

"Hey, no. You don't have to leave."

She turned back to face Dana. "You sound desperate. Jake must be your only option."

Dana nodded. "He's the only one I trust."

"Well then, you're in good hands."

"No," Jake said. "You're not going anywhere." He stepped up to Dana. "You want to talk to me, talk. But Lynn stays."

"It's about Hannah." Her eyes welled with tears.

He frowned. "Your sister? What about her?"

"She's been...Hannah's been..." Tears rolled down her face. "Hannah was murdered."

"My God. Dana, I'm so sorry."

"It's awful, Jake." She was sobbing. "Hannah didn't deserve to be gunned down like a mad dog."

"Of course not. But, Dana, why are you here? This is a job for the police, for homicide detectives."

"That's the problem. They arrested Aiden for her murder."

"Your brother-in-law? Nicest guy in the world? He would never even kill a spider."

"Aiden would never hurt Hannah, let alone kill her. I need you to find the real killer."

"Me? I'm not a homicide detective anymore. I run background checks, investigate missing persons, take pictures of cheating spouses. I don't work murder cases."

"Then Aiden's going to prison for the rest of his life." She sobbed into her hands.

Lynn heard the desperation in Dana's voice. She felt her pain. "Jake. There must be something you can do."

"The cops wouldn't have arrested him unless they had probable cause."

Lynn scowled at Dana. "What aren't you telling us?"

She exhaled slowly. "He was the last person to see her alive, took her home after dinner, then he went to play cards at an illegal gambling house, which gave him a shady alibi. When he got home, he found her body, called 911, and gave her CPR 'til the cops got there."

"Her blood was on his hands," Lynn put in.

"The cops don't buy his alibi."

Lynn could guess why. "Illegal gambling halls don't take names or videos, for obvious reasons."

"Case closed," Dana sobbed out.

Jake scoffed. "That's going to be a hard rap to beat."

"Jake, please." Dana sniffled. "He didn't do it."

"Even the nicest people can be pushed to their limit."

She let out an exasperated huff. "Come on, Jake. Once a detective, always a detective. Ignore the circumstantial evidence. Follow your instincts."

Lynn knew a thing or two about instincts. She placed her hand gently on Jake's arm. When he met her gaze, she gave him a nod. "Remember Drew's case. It wasn't what it appeared."

He looked at Dana. "Alright. I'll look into it."

"He always says that," Lynn said.

"Please, Jake. You need to help him."

"If I decide to take the case, I'll call you."

"How much?" she asked sheepishly.

"If you have to ask, you can't afford me."

"Fair enough." She reached into her purse and pulled out a business card. "Here's my cell number."

She walked out, still sobbing.

"I think you should take the case." Lynn sat in the chair.

"It doesn't work like that." Jake moved behind his desk and picked up his burger. "I've got to know what I'm getting into. Everything points to Aiden being the killer." He dropped the burger back down on the wrapper as if his appetite had gone south. "And what Dana didn't say is that Hannah has a history of infidelity. She probably had an affair, Aiden found out, and he snapped. Crime of passion. I'm not going to waste my time on a DA's slam dunk."

"There was evidence against Drew's sobriety. Common sense said he took off on a bender, but you took the case. Why not Dana's?"

He stared at his wilting burger. "I'm busy with cases. If I take Dana's..." A sly smile crossed his face as he looked up. "I'm going to need help. Someone smart, determined, with investigative instincts. Know anyone like that?" He winked at her.

"Really?"

"What better way to learn the P.I. business than from a professional with a desk-load of cases?"

Her heart flip-flopped with excitement. This was so sudden...she already had a lot on her plate, but what the hell? She decided to follow her heart.

"You've got yourself an assistant."

"And a gorgeous one at that."

"Don't forget pregnant." She held her hand out.

He accepted her hand, but instead of shaking it, he pulled her out of the chair, across the desk, and sealed the deal with a kiss.

Everything was falling into place. Her family was safe from Beth's wrath, her relationship with Jake was secure, they were happily pregnant, and she'd be getting hands-on work experience as a private investigator working on real cases. She felt relaxed, no longer focused on the *what-ifs* or the *maybes*. Now, she was eager to explore the joys her future had to offer.

What could possibly go wrong?

About the Author

Katelyn Marie Peterson graduated from Southern Connecticut State University with a bachelor's degree in journalism and writes freelance pieces for various newspapers. When she isn't typing on her laptop, she enjoys movie marathons, singing show tunes in the car, and cozying up with a good book. Katelyn resides in Connecticut with her husband and two children, a stay-at-home mom with a passion for writing Romance.

Katelyn Marie Peterson

Led by Her Heart

Also by Katelyn Marie Peterson

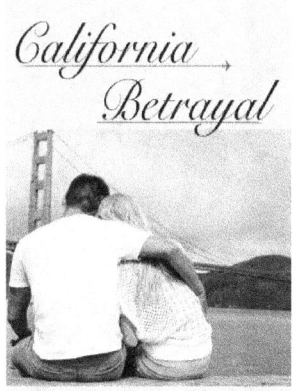

New York City transplant Shay Collins is apprehensive about returning to California for her brother's wedding. She knows she'll cross paths with her ex-husband, the drunk, and Jason, her secret high school flame and brother's best man, and she's excited to see her dad, her rock, but facing her manipulative mother is her biggest fear. True to form, Mom's got her nose in everyone's business, but when her brother's ex-girlfriend comes to town, Shay learns the depths of her mother's evil doings, and from there, it only gets worse as more lies are revealed. The wedding is off, her drunk ex is hospitalized after crashing his car, and Jason, the sweet man that he is, can't help her put out all the fires, but when her dad dies suddenly, one final betrayal comes to light, and that one is unforgivable. Through it all, Jason stands beside her, and the flames grow higher.

https://www.twbpress.com/californiabetrayal.html

Katelyn Marie Peterson

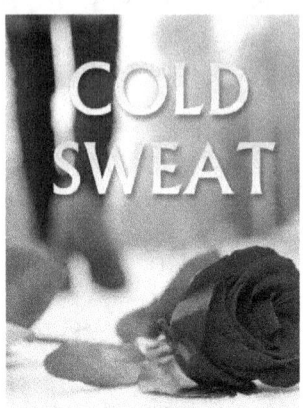

Isabel Kingston, a writer for a food magazine, is talking to her dad on the phone when he's killed by a mugger. On top of this trauma, the love of her life leaves town to make his fortune in the restaurant business, leaving her brokenhearted and bitter. The murder case goes cold, and she's plagued by nightmares in which her dying dad is trying to name his killer. She wakes up in a cold sweat. Is it possible the deceased can communicate with the living in their dreams? On the seventh anniversary of his murder, she's assigned to cover the story of a hometown restaurateur's return and the grand opening of his new eatery. Yes, it's her old flame, and he's come back to make amends, a move that rips open old wounds, upends her life, and drives a wedge between her and her present lover. It's as if the universe has turned against her, or perhaps it's divine intervention.

https://www.twbpress.com/coldsweat.html

Enjoy more short stories and novels by many talented authors at

https://www.twbpress.com

Science Fiction, Supernatural, Horror, Thrillers, Romance, and more

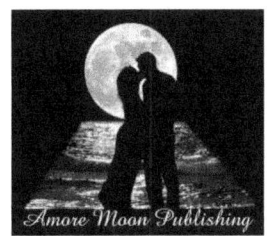

Amore Moon Publishing is an imprint of TWB Press.
www.twbpress.com/romance.html

Katelyn Marie Peterson

www.ingramcontent.com/pod-product-compliance
Lightning Source LLC
Chambersburg PA
CBHW071133260626
47162CB00003B/769